FOAL IN THE FOG

Mandy looked around wildly, expecting to see the smoking wreck of a car, but the road was empty. Just ahead of her, the wraithlike mist suddenly thinned. Mandy gasped as a skewbald foal came hurtling through the curtain of fog, its short tail flying out behind it. The thud of its unshod hooves on the road seemed deafening in the quiet. Mandy's heart hammered as she looked into the face of the foal. It slid to a halt and stared at her for a moment, lifting its small white nose. Its eyes were wide, and its nostrils flared as its sides heaved. And then the foal spun away up the side of the bank and streaked across the moor, vanishing as quickly as it had appeared.

Read more spooky Animal Ark™ Hauntings tales

Foal in the Fog

Ben M. Baglio

Illustrations by Ann Baum

Cover illustration by John Butler

AN
APPLE
PAPERBACK

SCHOLASTIC INC.

New York Toronto London Auckland Sydney
Mexico City New Delhi Hong Kong Buenos Aires

No part of this publication may be reproduced in whole or in part, or stored in
a retrieval system, or transmitted in any form or by any means, electronic,
mechanical, photocopying, recording, or otherwise, without written
permission of the publisher. For information regarding permission,
write to Working Partners Limited, 1 Albion Place, London W6 0QT,
United Kingdom.

ISBN 0-439-34415-8

Text copyright © 1999 by Working Partners Limited.
Original series created by Ben M. Baglio.
Illustrations copyright © 1999 by Ann Baum.

12 11 10 9 8 7 6 5   3 4 5 6 7/0

Printed in the U.S.A.   40

First Scholastic printing, May 2002

**Special thanks to Ingrid Maitland.
Thanks also to C. J. Hall,
B. Vet. Med., M.R.C.V.S., for reviewing
the veterinary information contained in this book.**

™

One

"And as the thunder crashed around them, the headless horseman streaked away across the moor. . . ."

"*Stop*, Dad." Mandy Hope groaned. "You're starting to give me the creeps with these stories."

"How do you know they're just *stories*?" Adam Hope teased, glancing at his daughter in the rearview mirror of the Land Rover. "They could be true."

"They're just local legends, Adam," said Mandy's mother. She sounded amused. "But they do help to pass the time."

Mandy grinned and nodded. The last hour of the trip had passed quickly. Out of the car window, her first im-

1

pression of Dartmoor was of a vast green wilderness, dotted with sheep and scattered boulders. But the mysterious legends of the place had held her spellbound. Her father's tales of evil pixies, vengeful ghosts, and skeleton steeds had fired her imagination as the dusk closed in, turning the moor around them to purple and black.

"How much longer?" she asked.

"About half an hour," Emily Hope replied. She held up the map. "Look, there's the village of Feston, and there's Whitehorse Hill, where the farm is — right in the middle of the moor."

There was a large blank space on the page where Mandy's mom was pointing. A few tiny roads were drawn across the expanse of moorland, but there were no towns or tourist centers. It looked like the perfect place for a pony trail-riding center.

"There's so much space for riding!" Mandy exclaimed. "I can't wait to get there."

Spring break had seemed slow in coming. In spite of a busy school term, the weeks leading up to their departure for Devon had crawled by for Mandy. Now she was tantalizingly close to seeing her second cousin Louise, as well as the ponies that belonged to Whitehorse Farm. She was starting to feel really excited.

Mandy loved animals. The thought of spending a

week surrounded by the sturdy little Dartmoor ponies was thrilling. Mandy's parents were both vets. They had a practice called Animal Ark at their home in the Yorkshire village of Welford. Mandy spent time in the busy clinic whenever she could, happily helping out. No task seemed too boring or distasteful to her.

"Ah!" Dr. Adam exclaimed, breaking into Mandy's thoughts. "There's the sign to the Gray Wethers, the twin rings of ancient stones I told you about." He was looking ahead to a weathered wooden signpost that pointed across the moor.

Mandy craned forward eagerly. "Is that the place where the shepherd and his flock were turned to stone?"

"That's right," said Dr. Emily. "The shepherd's beautiful wife, Felicity, ran away with a young nobleman, riding a magnificent horse."

"So he began to spend all his time with his sheep, because he was so lonely," Mandy finished. "And Hu, the god who lived on Sittaford Hill, turned him and his sheep into stones so they could never be parted from one another again."

Mandy stared out the window, trying to catch a glimpse of the stone circles. It was almost dark now, and it looked as though someone had dropped a giant piece of velvet cloth over the land.

In the front of the car, Dr. Emily began to smooth her

long auburn hair. Mandy put her sneakers back on and tied the laces. As she straightened up, she saw a large white sign with bold black writing, decorated with tiny horseshoes. "Whitehorse Farm Trekking Center," she read excitedly. "We're here!"

Dr. Adam eased the Land Rover through the two tall white gateposts. The farmhouse was at the end of a narrow road that ran slightly uphill. To her right, Mandy could see a cobblestone yard, edged with buildings that looked like stables, and she felt excitement welling up inside her. She rolled down the window and breathed deeply. On the warm night air was the scent of hay and horses. "It's fantastic," she breathed.

The road led to a low stone cottage. Dr. Adam honked the horn, and almost immediately a light came on above the front door. The house was illuminated, giving Mandy a chance to see its rose-pink walls and thatched roof. Louise's mother, Tracy, opened it and stepped out.

"Hello, Tracy!" Dr. Adam jumped out of the Land Rover and gave her a hug. The woman squeezed him tightly and then turned to Mandy and her mom.

"It's been such a long time since we've seen each other," Tracy said, smiling warmly at them both. "Good trip?"

"Yes, thanks. It's great to be at Whitehorse Farm. Is

Louise here?" Mandy smiled, looking around. She was longing to see her thirteen-year-old cousin — she hadn't seen her since Louise and her parents had come to stay with the Hopes in Welford, five years ago.

"She's at the stables," said Tracy as they followed her inside. "She'll be here in a moment. Well, come on into the kitchen, and we'll put the teakettle on. I've made sandwiches."

Tracy's husband, Mark, was sitting at the table in the warm, brightly lit kitchen. He was frowning over a pile of invoices and tapping numbers impatiently into a calculator. He looked up as they came in and pushed back his chair to stand up. "Adam, it's great to see you!" he said, shaking his cousin's hand. "And Emily!" He kissed her cheek. Then he gave Mandy a hug. She grinned at the tall, broad-shouldered man. She thought he looked exactly like her dad, his cousin. Just then, the door opened, and Louise, Mark and Tracy's daughter, came in.

"Hi, Mandy!" she said cheerfully.

"Hello," Mandy said, suddenly shy. Louise was now quite a bit taller than she was, and her curly brown hair was very short.

"We're going to have a great time while you're here." She grinned. "That is, if you like horses!"

"I love them," said Mandy, returning her smile.

"Lou, why don't you show Mandy the ponies before

bed?" Tracy suggested. "It's late, but I'm sure they won't mind a visitor!"

"Would you like to see them?" Louise asked Mandy.

Mandy's eyes were shining. "Now? Yes, please!" she said quickly.

Dr. Emily sank into a chair. "Go ahead. I'll just stay here and enjoy that cup of tea," she said.

"Tea sounds like a great idea to me," said Dr. Adam as he pulled out a chair beside his cousin. "We'll see you two later."

Louise led the way along a garden path to the stables Mandy had seen earlier. The cobblestone yard was neat and well swept, with a tidy muck heap in one corner.

"How many ponies do you have?" Mandy asked.

"Twelve," Louise answered. "They're all getting ready to work again now that it's spring."

"Twelve!" Mandy exclaimed.

"Lots of people come to ride, especially during the summer," Louise said, opening one of the doors to reveal a tack room that smelled invitingly of warm leather and saddle soap. "Not all of the ponies are stabled at night. Some are better outdoors in this warm weather." She flicked a switch just inside the door of the tack room, and the yard was suddenly brightly illuminated. A few curious heads appeared over stall doors. A bay-

colored pony in the nearest box nudged Mandy's arm, and she smoothed its sleek nose lovingly.

"They're gorgeous," she said. "They're not all Dartmoor ponies, are they?"

"We've got a couple of other breeds," Louise said, delving into her pocket for a tidbit. "We need some bigger horses for the adults to ride. But Dartmoors are best suited to life here. They've been roaming this moor for nearly a thousand years."

"How did they come to be on the moor in the first place?" asked Mandy, moving on to the next pony.

"Dartmoor was once a royal forest. King Henry I had one of the stallions brought to the royal stables for his own mares, and that's how the breed began," Louise explained.

"They were used to help in the mines later on, weren't they?" Mandy asked, remembering something from a history lesson.

"That's right." Louise nodded. "Tin mines. Because they were small and very strong, they made great pack ponies. Then the mines closed, and most of the ponies were turned loose onto the moor."

"To fend for themselves?" Mandy frowned.

"Yes, and they did very well. They're tough." Louise planted a kiss on the soft cheek of a chestnut pony. "Aren't you, Joe?" she added. The little pony lifted his nose and snorted, as if in agreement.

Mandy laughed. "He's great," she said.

"Would you like to go riding tomorrow?" asked Louise. "We could go out together."

"That would be wonderful." Mandy grinned, holding an outstretched hand to a gentle-looking gray mare. Her name, Cinders, was painted on a plaque on the stall door. She nuzzled Mandy's hand, then sniffed at her face with warm breath. The soft, long hairs on her muzzle tickled.

"May I ride Cinders?" Mandy asked Louise.

"Don't you want to meet all the other ponies before you decide?" Louise looked surprised.

"No, Cinders looks sweet," Mandy replied.

"She's a good choice," Louise said approvingly. "We'd better go. It's after eight."

Mandy gave the little gray mare a loving pat, then followed Louise back to the house. There were a billion bright stars in the sky, made all the more brilliant because the moor was so dark. Mandy could just make out the shapes of some ponies moving in the field. A few were standing by the fence, drawn there by the sound of their voices. She heard a soft whickering. *Tomorrow, I'll be out there*, Mandy thought, *riding Cinders*.

"Good night, all," Louise called out breezily. "See you tomorrow."

"See you tomorrow," Mandy echoed.

By the time they were in bed, the moon was shining through the open window of Louise's bedroom. Mandy stretched contentedly on her low cot, pulling the quilt up to her chin. She felt sleepy and full of sandwiches and hot chocolate. "You know, I love all the spooky stories about this moor," she began.

Louise yawned. "You've been hearing about the headless horses and the ghosts and things?"

"Yes," Mandy said. "Dad told me he'd read about a creature called the Dewer who stalked the moor with his huge black dog. Together they were supposed to have chased people over the cliffs and onto the jagged rocks below."

"Well," Louise said, her voice sounding sleepy, "I'm sure *you* don't believe in all that, do you? They're just stories, made up to frighten small children into being good."

"Maybe . . ." Mandy said thoughtfully.

There was no response from Louise's side of the room. Mandy presumed she'd fallen asleep. She felt very alone in the sudden silence but comforted by the pale moonlight filtering in through the open curtains. Then, all at once, the room became completely dark, as though someone had switched off the moon.

Mandy lay still, straining her ears. She had picked up the faintest moaning sound. It came eerily across the moor, a long way off, but she was certain of it. A prickle of fear made her shiver, and she drew up her knees and hugged them. There it was again! A long, low howl, faint but unmistakable. It had to be her imagination. . . .

The cloud that had covered the bright moon suddenly shifted, and the soft white light came in through the curtains once again. She saw Louise sleeping soundly in the bed beside hers and pushed the scary thoughts away. Tomorrow she would go riding. Mandy pulled the quilt over her ears and closed her eyes.

Two

Next morning, sunlight streamed in through the window, rousing Mandy from a dreamless sleep. She sat up and looked across at the next bed. It was empty and already neatly made. Jumping up, she made her own bed, then dressed quickly. In the cheerful little room, with the birds singing outside, her fears of the night before seemed silly. She'd been overtired, that was all — and overexcited, too!

Her mom and dad were in the kitchen, with Tracy and Mark.

"There's cereal and toast," Tracy announced as she

came in. "You've just missed Lou. She's gone down to see the ponies."

"Thanks," Mandy replied. "Can I just grab an apple and go join her?"

"Are you going to go riding, love?" Dr. Emily asked, looking at Mandy over the rim of her mug.

"Yep, can't wait." Mandy smiled, pinching a pile of buttered toast from her father's plate.

"You'll be careful, won't you?" Mark warned. "Did Louise tell you about the Dartmoor Stables?"

"The *what*?" Mandy frowned.

"Ah, the bogs!" Dr. Adam said. "'Dartmoor Stables' is the local name for bogs around here, Mandy."

"They're also called carpet bogs because the deep water is covered by soggy grass," Mark went on, through a mouthful of toast. "You need to watch out for them. You'll feel the ground start to wobble underneath you, and if you fall through, you'll find yourself swimming!"

"I'd better be careful, then," said Mandy. "Does Louise know where these bogs are?"

"She should by now," Tracy said cheerfully. "She's been riding this moor since she was four years old. She won't take you anywhere dangerous."

"I'll go find her, then," Mandy said, choosing an apple from a bowl on the table. "See you later."

"Take care!" Emily Hope called.

*   *   *

In the stable yard, Louise had already saddled Cinders and was tightening the girth on her own pony. "Hi, sleepyhead. I didn't want to wake you. You looked so peaceful," she said. "Come and meet Fern."

"Hi," Mandy replied. "She's lovely, Louise." The dark brown pony showed an interest in Mandy's half-eaten apple. Mandy took another big bite and offered Fern the rest of it, holding it out on the palm of her hand. Fern sniffed it for a moment, then snuffled it up with her whiskery lips.

"Okay," said Louise, giving Cinders's girth one last check. "Are you ready?"

"Ready!" Mandy took the reins and mounted. She smoothed the gray mare's sturdy neck affectionately as Cinders picked her way delicately across the cobblestones. The pony was gentle and patient, Mandy could tell. It felt good to be on Cinders's back, with the sun on her face and the whole of the moor stretched out in front of her. She twisted around in the saddle to look at Louise. "Where are we going first?"

"To Scorhill Stone Circle," her cousin replied. "It's a wonderful ride, and the weather's perfect."

"What *is* Scorhill Stone Circle?" Mandy asked as Fern and Cinders began to walk along a grassy trail that led between the fields beside the cottage.

"It's a circle of ancient stones," Louise answered. "No one knows exactly what they were used for, but it might be a sort of temple to worship the sun."

"That's amazing," Mandy said as they passed the field where the other ponies were grazing. "My dad told me about a circle where the story goes that a shepherd and his sheep were turned to stone."

Louise snorted. "You can believe what you like." She

grinned. "But they're nice to visit anyway." She urged Fern into a trot. Both ponies were fresh and eager. Beyond the gateposts lay hundreds of miles of granite and heather, crisscrossed by valleys and rivers.

"Your mom and dad said to be careful about the bogs," Mandy announced. "They sound dangerous!"

"Yes, they are," Louise agreed. "But I know what to look for, don't worry." She pressed Fern into a canter. Cinders needed no encouragement to follow. Mandy leaned forward in the saddle and buried her hands in Cinders's long gray mane. The little mare bounded along the track, her hooves thudding on the soft ground.

After a while, Louise slowed Fern to a walk. "Scorhill Circle's over there," she called to Mandy, pointing a little way ahead.

When Cinders had caught up to her, they approached the ancient site side by side, along a narrow lane overgrown with hedges. It opened out onto the moor, just a short distance from where the land suddenly hollowed out. Mandy could see the tops of the ancient stones.

There were twenty-four of them still standing — huge jagged slabs of solid rock, some of them shaped in a point. They were set in a wide, perfect circle in the ground, as though they had been carefully planted and had roots.

They walked closer. Mandy urged Cinders on toward the heart of the circle, but the pony was reluctant. She snorted, putting her nose to the ground.

"They don't like it here," Louise explained, slipping off Fern's back. "I don't know why. I think they find the stones a bit spooky."

"Oh," said Mandy, soothing her pony. Cinders walked hesitantly into the middle of the ring and stood still, her head held high as she looked warily around her. "How did they get here?" Mandy called to Louise wonderingly. "They're huge!"

"It's a mystery," smiled Louise, walking over and giving Cinders a mint. "Lots of people have tried to figure it out. And they're not the only stone circles on Dartmoor, you know. Some are even bigger than this one. There are rows of stones, and single standing stones, and even stone crosses."

"Wow," Mandy breathed, trying to imagine life on the moor as it was lived several thousand years before. "There might have been a village here once, with huts and animals and everything."

"People say that if a woman was suspected of being a witch she would be brought to the circle on midsummer night," Louise said. "She would be made to wash in Cranmere Pool, not far from here, and then to run around Scorhill Stone Circle three times. Then she had to kneel down, facing the stones. If the stones stayed upright, she was set free. If they fell on top of her, the woman was supposed to be guilty."

"Ugh!" cried Mandy. "How horrible!" She got down and looked at the gaps in the circle where the fallen stones lay embedded in the earth and shuddered. Cinders seemed to notice and stepped restlessly sideways.

"Anyway," Louise went on, "I think it's all a lot of nonsense."

Mandy gazed at the impressive stones, her imagination aflame. She didn't find it so easy to dismiss the old stories.

Louise put the reins back over Fern's head. "Come on," she said, putting her foot in the stirrup. "Let's go a bit farther. Do you want to see the Tolman Stone?"

"Yes, please," Mandy said, swinging up into the saddle. She couldn't get enough of the strange legends of this haunting moor. As they walked out of the circle, Cinders shied away from one of the Scorhill stones. Mandy touched her lightly with her heels. "It's okay," she said, patting her neck.

She followed Louise downhill toward the sloping banks of the Teign, a shallow river that sparkled in the sunlight as it splashed over the rocks that lay on the peaty brown riverbed.

"There. See it?" Louise pointed.

Mandy looked ahead of them and saw a towering stone sticking up out of the water. It was a granite block more than a yard thick, and the running water had worn a large, smooth hole right through its center.

"It's amazing," Mandy said.

"Do you have any aches and pains?" asked Louise teasingly.

"Aches and pains?" Mandy was puzzled.

Louise laughed. "Well, if you get into the river and haul yourself through the hole in the stone, you'll be healed! That's what they *say*, anyway."

"Really?" Mandy chuckled. She studied the narrow, sharply angled hole. "It wouldn't be very easy!"

"It certainly wouldn't," Louise agreed. "Now come on, we'd better start back, if you're ready." She checked her watch.

"Sure." Mandy turned Cinders to face the way they had come. "Do you always ride Fern?" she asked as the ponies started back up the hill.

"Fern and Merry are my favorites," Louise admitted. "But I love all of our ponies."

"It must be great, living here," Mandy said. "It's so . . . wild!"

"It *is* great." Louise nodded. "Only I'm away at school during most of the year. And during the summer the place is alive with tourists."

"Isn't that fun?" Mandy looked sideways at her.

"It can be." Louise made a face. "But then there are always the ones who don't know one end of a pony from the other."

Mandy laughed.

"So what do you want to be when you're older?" Louise asked.

"A vet," Mandy said, without hesitation. "What about you?"

"I don't really know," said Louise. "Except that it will be something to do with horses," she added. She reached down and petted Fern's neck lovingly.

Mandy looked out over the emptiness of the moor. The sky was beginning to cloud over, and the hills on the horizon were veiled in mist. The air felt much cooler now that the sun was behind clouds. From time to time Mandy noticed squelchy little hollows in the ground. She wondered if these were mini versions of the treacherous bogs.

Louise glanced up at the clouds gathered overhead and gave Fern a nudge with her heels. The little pony tossed her head and broke into a canter. Mandy shortened her reins and followed them across the moor. When she reached a narrow wooden footbridge that led over a deep gully, Louise reined in Fern and turned around to watch Mandy and Cinders race over the hill.

Mandy was flushed and slightly out of breath when she pulled up beside her cousin. "That was great!" she said, leaning forward to pat Cinders's hot neck.

Louise smiled at her. "We can ride every day while you're here, if you want to."

"I'd love to," Mandy said firmly.

"This bridge is a shortcut," Louise explained. "It looks like the weather's closing in, so we ought to get going." She turned Fern toward the bridge and squeezed the pony with her legs. Fern took a few steps toward the entrance to the bridge, then hesitated. He stood still, peering nervously into the gully. "Come on, boy. It's only a bridge!"

But Fern planted his forelegs firmly on the grassy bank. He looked from side to side, as though he was trying to decide whether to bolt into the river and up the other side of the bank.

"Uh-oh," Mandy said softly. She sensed trouble. Fern seemed determined not to go across the bridge.

"Steady there, boy," Louise soothed. "You're all right." She squeezed her legs again, but this time Fern took a few steps backward, away from the bridge.

"Let me go across," Mandy suggested. "Fern might feel happier to follow if he sees Cinders cross."

"Okay." Louise frowned. "I don't know what's gotten into him."

Mandy quickly walked Cinders across the wooden planks of the bridge. The gray mare stepped very cautiously, but she seemed to trust Mandy enough to cross. On the other side, Mandy turned Cinders to face Louise. Fern's ears were back, and he dug at the earth with one hoof and danced around in a circle.

"Fern!" Louise scolded, frustrated. "What *is* the matter with you!"

Mandy looked around for another way across the river. She was surprised to see that mist had come rolling across the moor in a great swath of gray and white, swirling silently closer. "Lou!" Mandy called. "Look!"

Louise had dismounted and was trying to lead Fern across the bridge. She made a face when she saw how close the mist was. "The fog's nearly here. We need to get going," she said.

"What do you think we should do?" Mandy called, facing Louise across the river. The first tendrils of mist had reached them by now, and Louise and Fern looked gray and blurry.

"You go on ahead, Mandy," Louise shouted. "We'd better not hang around with this fog coming in. We're not far from home. Stick to the riverbank. I won't be far behind you. I'll just try to calm Fern down and get him across this bridge."

"But what will you do if Fern refuses?" Mandy called.

"I'll take him around the other way." Louise pointed back the way they had come. "It's a bit longer, that's all. Don't worry, we'll be fine. Go."

"All right," Mandy shouted back, "if you're sure."

"I'm sure," Louise called. "Cinders will take you home. Just let her take you along the bank of the river."

Mandy shortened her reins and spoke to Cinders, who was shifting restively. "Come on, girl," she said softly. "Take me home."

Three

As Mandy followed the left bank of the Teign, the ground quickly became squelchy and soft underfoot. Mud sucked at Cinders's hooves, and from time to time the little mare stopped to nibble at a tuft of grass.

"No time for a snack," Mandy told her, pulling the pony's head up. She allowed Cinders to pick her own way, checking to make sure the river was on their right. Walking gingerly through the thickening mist, Cinders took her down a short slope and toward a clump of dark, shadowy trees. As they drew closer, the trunks loomed up through the mist, suddenly sharp in focus.

"I don't remember seeing these trees before," Mandy

said, her voice sounding loud in the mist-laden silence. She realized that she could no longer hear the familiar gurgling of the river water. Mandy drew Cinders to a halt and looked around her. She began to feel a little nervous. The gully was no longer beside them. "Go ahead, Cinders," she urged, nudging her with her heels. "Home!"

The pony walked on, but Mandy could tell she was hesitant. The mist pressed in on them, leaving Mandy's face damp and cold. She used her sleeve to wipe her cheeks and upper lip. Beyond the trees, she looked hopefully for a landmark — a house, a road, something. Drifting clouds had settled low across the moor, and with a start, Mandy realized she had completely lost her sense of direction. Where had they parted from the river?

"Louise isn't far behind," she announced to the pony, trying to keep their spirits up. But the moor, so beautiful in the spring sunlight earlier that morning, now seemed a desolate place. It was colorless and chilly, and under the shadow of low clouds it almost felt unfriendly.

Mandy listened, hoping to hear the faint sound of Fern's approach or Louise's call. Nothing. Even the birds were silent. Cinders slowed to a stop and sniffed the damp air. She shifted around, her ears twitching.

"Oh, no," said Mandy to the pony, finally facing the truth. They were lost. "What do we do now, girl?"

Cinders snorted and stamped her hoof. There was nothing to go on, no clue to tell them which way to go. The mist enveloped them completely. The moor seemed to have drifted away, leaving Mandy and her pony stranded in a sea of dense cloud. She sat still, holding the reins slack, trying to take comfort from the warmth of Cinders's flanks through her jodhpurs. There was no way of knowing how far they had strayed from the river, but she couldn't risk striking out deeper across the moor. The thought of plunging into one of the dreaded carpet bogs was enough to help Mandy make up her mind.

"We'll have to head back the way we've come," she announced to Cinders. "We need to try to find the river again."

Mandy peered at the ground for signs of Cinders's hoofprints as they walked along. They were easily visible in places, but in others the soggy brown earth had swallowed up all traces. The few Mandy could see led her back to the clump of trees they had passed earlier, and her spirits rose. "We're not very far from the river now," she said aloud. Feeling happier, she opened her mouth to sing a song she'd learned recently for the school play, but she shut it again quickly. She'd heard a noise that, at first, she couldn't place. Mandy pulled Cinders to a halt and listened. It was the rumble of wheels on a road. She'd been listening for the sound of the river. The hum of a car's engine was the last thing she'd expected to hear. "It's a car!" she cried. "We must be near a road. If we hurry, we can ask them for directions."

She pressed her heels into the pony's sides and faced her in the direction of the noise. Cinders broke into a trot. Mandy aimed toward the sound. She and Cinders got to the top of a hill, where the mist was thinner. She could just make out a slope of butter-yellow gorse and a granite mound to the left. A ribbon of road snaked away in front of her. Turning her head from side to side, she looked for the car, but it was nowhere to be seen.

And then there was a terrifying squeal of brakes, lasting several seconds. Shock clutched at Mandy's heart. She hunched her shoulders and covered her ears.

The sound of metal being ripped apart came ringing across to her, along with the splintering crash of breaking glass. An acrid smell of burning rubber filled her nostrils.

"Oh, no!" Mandy gasped. The silence that followed the crash was more frightening than anything else. She longed for footsteps, a shout, even a cry for help. She strained to see the accident. The mist seemed to have gotten thicker again, making it impossible to see anything. She gathered her courage and dismounted, reasoning that she would be more able to help on her feet.

"Wait for me, girl," she said. "I'll be back." She looped Cinders's reins around a branch of prickly gorse, her hands trembling with shock. It had sounded like a terrible crash. Would anyone be injured? Mandy gave Cinders a quick pat and set off down the slope toward the road.

As she ran, she stumbled over sharp stones, glossy green with moss, her arms outstretched against any unseen obstacles in the mist. "I'm coming! I'll help you," she shouted, reaching the road.

She looked around wildly, expecting to see the smoking wreck of a car, but the road was empty. Just ahead of her, the wraithlike mist suddenly thinned. Mandy gasped as a skewbald foal came hurtling through the curtain of fog, its short tail flying out behind it. The thud of its unshod hooves on the road seemed deafening in the quiet. Mandy's heart hammered as she looked into the face of the foal. It slid to a halt and stared at her for a moment, lifting its small white nose. Its eyes were wide, and its nostrils flared as its sides heaved. And

then the foal spun away up the side of the bank and streaked across the moor, vanishing as quickly as it had appeared.

Mandy was rooted to the spot. Maybe the foal had been traveling in the vehicle she'd just heard crash!

Cinders's warm breath nuzzling her hand made her jump. The mare's reins must have come loose, and she had made her way down to the road to find Mandy.

She reached out to reassure her with a gentle stroke. "Come on, girl," she said gingerly, swinging up into the saddle. "We'd better take a closer look."

At Mandy's urging, Cinders set off up the road at a brisk trot. A breeze had sprung up, blowing the mist away. Mandy sensed that Cinders was happier now that the way ahead was clear. But there was still the scene of the accident to be found. Peering to each side, Mandy followed the road in one direction, then turned and headed back the other way. But there was no sign of a car — no tire marks scorched into the earth, no signs of the grassy shoulders of the road having been torn up by a vehicle veering out of control.

Strange, Mandy thought. And what about the foal? What if it was injured? It had seemed okay, but it was definitely frightened. It could so easily get lost on the vast moor. Maybe she should try to find it. But it was dangerous, rushing off across an unknown stretch of moor that might be studded with carpet bogs.

Mandy slowed Cinders and caught her breath. She had to avoid getting lost a second time, now that she had managed to find the road. She needed to get home to organize a search party to find the car that had crashed.

"Which way?" Mandy asked Cinders. There was a rumble of thunder overhead. Cinders hesitated for a moment, then she turned right and set off at a brisk walk. "I hope you know where you're going this time," Mandy said, patting the pony.

At least the mist along the road was lifting, and as they made their way forward Mandy felt a little easier. There was a second roll of thunder, and the first drops of rain began to fall. She listened to the sound of Cinders's hooves striking the pavement in the silence and thought about Louise. Had she managed to get Fern to go across the narrow bridge? Perhaps she was already back at Whitehorse Farm, wondering what on earth had happened to Mandy and Cinders.

Just then, she heard the sound of an approaching car. Mandy steered Cinders onto the shoulder. She waited, watching the oncoming beams, then waved her hands in the air to get their attention. At last, headlights were on her, blinding her, and the car stopped. It was being driven by her dad's cousin, Mark.

"Mandy!" Dr. Adam emerged from the passenger seat and bounded forward through the rain. "Are you all right?"

Relief flooded through Mandy. She slipped off Cinders's back and hugged her father. "I'm fine, Dad, but I left Louise ages ago. She —"

"Louise is back at the farm," Dr. Adam said quickly. "She's fine."

"Oh, good!" Mandy sighed, looking relieved. "I must have taken a wrong turn somewhere. I lost sight of the river. And then the weirdest thing happened."

"Well, thank heavens you're okay," Mark said briskly, interrupting her. "Look, I have to get the car off the road. It's dangerous parked where it is."

"Dad!" Mandy pulled urgently at his sleeve. "Listen. I think there's been an accident. I heard the sound of a car crashing. And there was a foal, running down the road. I don't know if it was in the accident or just frightened. But when I looked for a car, I couldn't see anything."

"Mark!" Dr. Adam called out as his cousin came back toward them, holding a large red umbrella. "Mandy thinks there's been an accident. We'd better look around."

"I heard it happening," Mandy said, "but I haven't been able to find a car along this road."

"Really?" Mark looked concerned. "Are you sure?"

"Yes." Mandy nodded, frowning. "I definitely heard a sound — like someone slamming on brakes, then a crash."

"We'd better hurry," Mark said. "Come on." He turned to go back up the road.

"It was foggy," Mandy went on, her words tumbling out, "so I might have missed it. There might be a ditch or something."

Mandy's father looked alarmed. "Mark and I will have a look. But it doesn't sound like we can do anything about the foal now. Let's hope it was a wild pony who just got scared by the crash. You'd better head back — the farm's about a mile from here, straight along this road."

"Okay." Mandy mounted Cinders. Her coat was hot and damp, and her head drooped. They set off at a gentle walk along the edge of the road. It was still raining heavily, and water dripped down the back of Mandy's neck. The sound of the squealing brakes played over and over again in her head, followed by the eerie silence and the sudden sound of thudding hooves. Mandy hoped desperately that the foal was okay. She again saw the animal's pleading dark eyes in the fog.

The gates of Whitehorse Farm were just coming into view when Mark's car pulled up alongside Cinders. "Did you find anything?" Mandy asked.

"Nothing," said her father, opening the passenger window to talk to her. "No sign of a car anywhere." He shrugged.

"Are you absolutely certain you heard a crash?" Mark asked gently, looking over at Mandy from the driver's seat.

"Absolutely," Mandy replied.

"It might have been the thunder," he suggested.

"No," said Mandy, shaking her head. "No, it didn't sound like thunder." She flinched as the horrifying sound filled her mind again. "I definitely heard a crash. I couldn't have imagined it."

"Well, you take Cinders back to the stable," Mark told her. "I'll drive around again, if that will make you feel better."

"Yes, please!" Mandy said worriedly. "And keep a look out for the foal as well. It was a skewbald with a white stripe on its nose." Her heart tightened as she pictured the foal's terrified face.

"Okay," Mark said. "We'll see you later." He swung the car around and headed back down the narrow road.

Mandy felt her shoulders droop in defeat. It had been frighteningly real. Why was there no trace of the car or its driver? Mandy felt a little chill begin to travel up her spine. She shivered, then pulled herself together. She had been so distracted by the mysterious accident that she had momentarily forgotten her tired, wet pony.

Mandy led Cinders into the stable yard, where she found Louise mucking out one of the stalls.

"Oh, Mandy! Are you okay?" Louise looked worried. "I'm sorry you got lost. It must have been awful!"

"I'm okay," Mandy answered, managing to smile. "I was worried about *you*!"

"I thought you'd make it if you stuck to the river-bank," Louise went on, shaking her head.

"The mist was so thick, I couldn't really *see* the river-bank!" Mandy said. "Still, there's no harm done. Cinders was great. Can I give her some feed?"

"Sure. I've made some bran mash, for a special treat. She looks as though she deserves it!" Louise said.

As Mandy unsaddled Cinders, she told her cousin about the sound of the car crash and how she hadn't been able to find anything.

"That's strange." Louise looked puzzled. "Are you sure? About what you heard, I mean?"

Mandy nodded. "Yes, I'm sure."

"Well, anyway," Louise said, "if there *was* an accident, it's been taken care of by now. Someone must have called an ambulance."

"Yes," Mandy agreed, feeling comforted by Louise's words. She made up her mind not to say anything about the appearance of the foal. Louise had sounded as doubtful as her father and Mark about the accident, and she didn't want everyone to think she had a wild imagination.

"You look exhausted!" Louise said suddenly. "Why don't you go up to the house and get my mom to give you something to eat? I'll finish up here."

"Okay," Mandy replied. "I'll just put Cinders away." She turned Cinders loose in her stall and gave her a pat. Then she walked slowly back to the house, her thoughts whirling. She had definitely heard the squeal of a car's brakes, followed by a crash. She *couldn't* have imagined it! And then there had been the little skewbald foal cantering through the mist. Mandy was certain she hadn't imagined that, either. She paused at the garden gate and looked out across the moor. Even though the rain had stopped, the sky was dark and heavy, and the moor looked cold and forbidding. Mandy pictured the terrified foal, hurtling across the treacherous ground. Would she be all right?

Four

"I telephoned the police last night," Mark told Mandy the next day when she caught up with him on her way down to the stable. "Just to make sure. But there were no reports of a car accident around this area yesterday."

"Oh," said Mandy. "Well, thanks for checking."

"I just wanted to put your mind at ease," Mark added. He opened the gate to the yard and stepped aside to let Mandy go first. Two ponies tethered to a rail looked up expectantly. One of them, a beautiful bay, gave a shrill whinny.

Louise was hosing down the yard. She was wearing

a pair of Wellingtons, tall boots worn on farms, and a hat to keep the sun off her face. After yesterday's fog and rain, the sky had cleared and the sun shone down fiercely.

Louise looked up. "Hi there." She aimed the jet of water at the trough.

"A lot of bookings today, Lou," Mark called from the door of the office. He had a large appointment book in his hands.

"Yeah, they'll be here soon," Louise replied. "The first of the season."

"Riders?" Mandy asked.

"Yes." Louise nodded, putting a bridle on the bay pony. "Two children and their mother, I think."

"Can I help?" Mandy offered.

"Yes, please," Louise answered. "Can you pick out Montana's feet? He's the chestnut with the white face in that stall over there."

Mandy went into the tack room and rummaged about for a hoof pick. She couldn't help thinking about the foal she had seen on the moor. If there really hadn't been a car accident, then what had frightened it? She remembered the way it had bolted past her into the fog, and her heart clenched with anxiety.

"Did you find a pick, Mandy?" Louise called, disturbing her thoughts.

"Yes, I'm coming," she answered, spotting a red hoof pick in a box of grooming things.

Mark was saddling Moonlight, the pretty bay who had been chosen for the younger child. Pecan, a stocky roan who was tied next to Moonlight, stretched out and nudged him for a treat.

"Hey," said Mark warningly. "Back, Pecan. Don't be greedy." There was a jealous squeal and a show of teeth. "Can you put Pecan's saddle on, please, Mandy?"

"Sure," Mandy said happily, emerging from Montana's stall. She loved being here in the stable yard with the ponies.

She stayed around, helping where she could, until the Shaw family who had booked to go riding arrived by car. Charles, who was ten, mounted Pecan, and his eight-year-old sister was given a leg up onto Moonlight. Louise had saddled up Fern for their mother to ride. Mark was going to accompany the Shaws on Harvey, his long-legged chestnut Thoroughbred.

"Have a great morning," Louise called cheerfully as the four riders set out toward the gateposts.

Mrs. Shaw waved her map in reply. "Thank you!" she said.

"Nice weather," Mandy remarked, watching them head onto the moor from her vantage point on a bale of hay. "Not like yesterday."

"Yes," Louise agreed, adding teasingly, "let's hope they don't come across any headless horses, witches — or even a crashed car!"

Mandy felt herself blush as Louise laughed.

"Come on," Louise nudged her in the ribs. "I'll take you over to meet my friend Abby. She lives on the farm on the other side of Whitehorse Hill. She's crazy about horses, too."

"Great!" Mandy jumped up, her brief embarrassment forgotten. "Can we ride there?"

"Of course. Take whoever you want." Louise smiled. "Come on, let's go."

Mandy chose Montana over Cinders. After the rigors of yesterday, she felt the little mare deserved a day in the field, grazing in the sunshine.

As she and Louise trotted along a lane edged with tangled, overgrown hedges, they chatted easily about the different ponies at the center. Mandy was forced to duck low over Montana's withers to avoid the overhanging branches. The dirt road was soft and muddy from yesterday's rain, and the ponies seemed pleased to be out.

It didn't take them long to reach Sittaford Farm, which lay in a narrow valley between Whitehorse Hill and Sittaford Tor. At first, the yard appeared to be empty. The gray stone buildings seemed quiet and deserted. Then Montana shied as shrill barking rang out across the cobbled courtyard. Around the corner came a black-and-white Border collie, yapping furiously.

"Silly old Domino," Louise said. "It's me. Where's your owner? Abby, where are you?" she called.

Mandy dismounted and led Montana to the water trough in the yard. The collie rushed to her and put up a front paw to be shaken. Mandy laughed and patted his thick fur affectionately.

"I'm here." A blond-haired girl about Mandy's age appeared in the doorway to a small office. She had a magazine in her hands. "Oh, it's you, Lou. Hi."

Mandy's first thought was that the girl didn't look very pleased to see them. She had a nervous look on her face and stood biting her nails, refusing to make eye contact.

"This is Mandy Hope," Louise announced. "My second cousin. She's come from Yorkshire to stay for a week."

"Hello." Abby smiled halfheartedly. Mandy took another look at her. On second appearance, it seemed as though the girl had a shy, gentle manner. She smiled back. "Hi."

"Cody's had pups," Abby told Louise hesitantly. She glanced across the yard to the farmhouse.

"Oh, *great*! Cody is Abby's Labrador," Louise explained to Mandy.

"Wow! Can we see them?" asked Mandy.

"If you like," Abby replied, without looking at Mandy. "They're up at the house. Come on."

Mandy and Louise tied their ponies to metal rings set in the wall of one of the outbuildings. Then they followed Abby across the yard and into the farmhouse. Abby shut the door behind them, telling Domino to stay outside.

The puppies were by the stove in the kitchen, in a large cardboard box. They were curled up together, asleep. Four of them were yellow and one was pitch-black.

"Oh, they're absolutely gorgeous!" Mandy sighed, sinking to her knees beside the box.

"How *cute*!" Louise exclaimed. "Can we pet them, Abby?"

"Sure," she said. "Cody doesn't seem to mind them being picked up."

"Cody's the mother," Louise filled Mandy in. "And Coco's the father. He belongs to Abby, too."

Mandy eagerly reached into the box, gently lifting a tiny pup into her arms. She breathed in the milky smell of its warm little body. The puppy's eyes were closed.

"Oh, you're *so* lovely!" she murmured, pressing her lips against its silky head.

"When were they born, Abby?" Louise asked. She had picked up the puppy with the dark coat and was smoothing its tiny head with one finger.

"Um . . . the day before yesterday," Abby answered. She walked restlessly to the window and stood with her back to Mandy as she spoke. Mandy was surprised at how withdrawn she seemed. Perhaps Abby didn't much like dogs, she reasoned.

A golden-haired Labrador appeared at the kitchen door. She hurried over to her litter, looking anxious.

"Here's Cody," Louise said. "Hello, girl!"

"Hello, you clever girl." Mandy put her hand out to the dog, who sniffed her fingers. Cody climbed into the box and settled down very carefully in order to not squash any of her puppies. Mandy immediately put the puppy in beside her, and it began to search for milk.

Louise did the same. "What a good mom you are," she remarked. "Isn't she, Abby?"

Abby just shrugged. "I suppose so," she said.

Mandy was puzzled. Abby seemed so sad and somehow troubled. What could be the matter? If the puppies had been in her kitchen at Animal Ark, Mandy knew she would be beside herself with excitement. She would ask Louise if anything was wrong as soon as she could. Louise was Abby's friend and she had to know. Mandy watched Abby stare out the window, a tense, nervous expression on her face.

"What's so interesting out there?" Louise went over to the window and joined her friend. She peered out at the garden, resting her hand on Abby's shoulder.

"Nothing!" Abby shrugged off Louise's hand and turned away from the window. "I'm just looking, that's all."

"Well, why don't we take the ponies down to the river?" Louise suggested brightly. Mandy could tell she was trying to cheer up her friend.

"You go," Abby said. "I promised my mom I'd finish my homework."

"Oh, Abby," Louise sighed. "You never come out with the ponies anymore. I miss you!"

"Yes, please come," urged Mandy. "It'd be nice to have you with us, Abby. Are you sure you can't spare an hour?"

"I'm sure," Abby said. "But thanks anyway," she added, not meeting their eyes.

"Okay. Mandy and I will go and get Montana and Toffee," Louise said. "Work hard!"

"Thanks," Abby said. The troubled expression had returned to her face.

Mandy smiled at her, then turned to leave.

"Thanks for coming, Mandy," Abby said suddenly, in a small voice.

"Thanks for letting me see your puppies. Bye, Abby," Mandy said. "I hope you get your homework done soon."

As they walked back across the yard, Mandy fell into step beside Louise. "Why wouldn't she come with us?" she asked, feeling puzzled. "I mean, she could've done her project tomorrow."

"Oh, that's Abby for you!" Louise shrugged. Then she began to run. "Now, come on, let's untie those ponies before Toffee chews through his bridle!"

*   *   *

Louise rode hard across the moor, heading for a shallow river. Mandy stayed close behind her, grateful for the clear blue sky and the sunshine. It was so much nicer riding when you could actually see where you were going! When Louise finally stopped, it was beside a meandering stretch of water, shallow enough for the ponies to stand in.

"Phew!" Mandy dismounted and took off her riding hat. "It's hot." She led Montana to the river's edge, and he drank with long, thirsty gulps. Toffee seemed content just to stand in the shade of an overhanging tree, the water rushing around his hooves. Mandy peeled off her sweater and lay back on the grass, feeling the soft blades tickle her skin through her T-shirt. "Hmm, this is nice," she said. "It would have been nice if Abby had come with us, too. Why wouldn't she come? Do you know?"

Louise sat down beside Mandy on the grass. She shrugged. "She's been acting really weird lately."

"How do you mean, weird?" Mandy was puzzled.

"Well, something really bad happened to her a couple of months ago," Louise began. "She's been acting strange ever since then."

Mandy sat up and looked at Louise. "What sort of thing?" she urged.

"Well." Louise hesitated, plucking restlessly at the

grass beside her. "You wouldn't know it now, but Abby is crazy about horses. Four months ago, her parents bought her a foal for her birthday. It was a skewbald, ten months old. Abby named her Curiosity. She just adored her."

"Yes?" Mandy prompted. "Then what?"

"Abby was driving with her dad in the truck one day. Curiosity was in the trailer. They were on their way to Chagford, to see the vet. Abby told me that her dad was listening to football on the radio, so she asked him to tune in to something less boring."

Mandy frowned as Louise paused. "Go on," she said encouragingly.

"Abby's dad began fiddling around, trying to change the radio station. He must have taken his eyes off the road for a second because —"

"Oh, no," Mandy gasped, covering her mouth with her hands.

"A car came around the corner in the opposite direction," Louise went on. "Mr. Taylor swerved, and the truck skidded off the road."

"Oh," said Mandy, horrified. "Not her *dad* . . ."

"No." Louise shook her head. "Not Abby's dad. He was all right, and so was she. Just a bit bruised. But the trailer overturned."

"Curiosity!" Mandy exclaimed. Her heart thudded

painfully in her chest, and she suddenly felt cold in spite of the sunshine.

"The ramp fell down, and Curiosity fell out," Louise explained. "She must have panicked because she galloped off across the moor. It was a foggy day, and even though Abby and her dad went after her, they couldn't find her."

"Oh, Lou," said Mandy sadly. "How horrible! So is Abby still worried about her lost foal?"

"No." Louise shook her head. "This is the saddest part. Abby searched the moor, looking for her. She wouldn't give up. She knew Curiosity was out there somewhere and that she would find her eventually. Then, two days later, she did."

"Oh, but where? How?" Mandy asked.

"Curiosity had fallen into a bog," Louise said, her face a picture of misery. "She had died trying to escape." Louise got up and walked toward the trunk of the tree. She leaned against it, looked out sadly across the moor.

Mandy couldn't speak. It was one of the saddest stories she'd ever heard. No wonder poor Abby was heartbroken.

"Abby blames herself for Curiosity's death," Louise went on. "She says that if she hadn't distracted her dad while he was driving, the accident wouldn't have happened."

"Poor Abby," said Mandy softly.

"She's really changed since it happened," Louise said, frowning. "She used to be so much fun. Now she doesn't want to go out much. I can't get her to go riding at all. If she goes to the yard, she just sits in the farm office and won't help with any of the other animals on the farm."

"She did seem very unhappy," Mandy agreed. "Sort of closed off from the world."

"Well, anyway," Louise said briskly, brushing down her jodhpurs and looking around for her hat, "I don't suppose there's anything anyone can do. She'll have to get over it in her own time. We'd better start back, okay?"

"Yes, okay." Mandy got to her feet and went into the water to fetch Montana. The pony was reluctant to leave the cold water, and Mandy had to tug on the reins. Looking across the river's shimmering surface, Mandy noticed Montana's watery reflection. The shimmering outline of his white, striped face in the water reminded her of the little skewbald she had seen in the mist on the moor the day before. What a coincidence that Abby's beloved Curiosity had been a skewbald, too. But maybe it wasn't a coincidence.

As she led Montana up the bank, Mandy thought again about the foal's sudden appearance in the fog yesterday. Perhaps Curiosity *hadn't* died, after all. Perhaps she was running wild on the moor.

"Louise," she said, mounting Montana, "it was definitely Curiosity that Abby found in the bog, wasn't it? I mean, she's absolutely sure of that? It couldn't have been another skewbald foal, could it?"

"Of course not!" Louise said. "Abby would know her own foal, wouldn't she? Why?"

"Oh, nothing," Mandy said. "I just wondered." She touched her heels to her pony's sides. Louise would probably think she was crazy if she suggested that Curiosity was still roaming around Dartmoor, so Mandy decided not to say anything. But she couldn't get the foal out of her mind.

Five

Mandy spent Sunday morning helping Louise in the yard. It was warm and sunny, and great clouds of dust rose from the ponies' thick coats as Mandy groomed them. Montana leaned his head drowsily against her back as she picked out his feet.

"You're really good with horses," Louise commented as she spread clean straw in Montana's stable.

"Thanks," Mandy said. "I used to go help at our local stables when I was learning to ride."

Just then a car pulled up. Mrs. Taylor, Abby's mother, climbed out and waved to them. "Hello there," she called, opening the gate and walking across the yard.

"Hi, Mrs. Taylor," Louise answered cheerfully. "What can we do for you? By the way, this is Mandy, my second cousin."

"Hello, Mandy." Mrs. Taylor smiled. "I was just passing on my way back from Feston, Louise. I wanted to talk about Abby."

"Oh," said Lou. She stopped what she was doing and gave Abby's mom her full attention.

"Is Abby here?" Mandy asked, looking past Mrs. Taylor to the gate.

"She's in the car." Mrs. Taylor looked down for a moment before starting again. "Louise, has Abby said anything to you about the way she's feeling? She's been so quiet lately, even more so than she was just after the accident. We wondered if you might know if there's anything else troubling her."

"No, I'm sorry." Louise shook her head. "She hasn't mentioned anything to me."

"Oh, dear." Mrs. Taylor looked worried.

"She does seem to be very sad about Curiosity still," Mandy ventured, hoping she wasn't speaking out of turn. "Louise told me what happened. I'm really sorry."

"Thank you, Mandy." Mrs. Taylor nodded. "We need to try to do something to help her through all this. I wondered if you would try to get her to go riding with you again. I'm sure it would do her good."

"We'd love her to come along," Louise said emphatically. "If we can persuade her, that is. Wouldn't we, Mandy?"

"Oh, yes," Mandy said. "Of course!"

"Well, maybe tomorrow, if you're going out," said Mrs. Taylor. "You might make a world of difference. Thanks, both of you."

"That's okay," Louise said. "Leave it to us."

As Mrs. Taylor hurried out of the yard, Mandy picked up a soft body brush and began brushing Montana's tail. She listened to the car start and drive away and thought about Abby. "The thing I wonder, Louise," she began, "is why Abby is feeling *worse*. After all, it's been quite a few weeks since Curiosity died."

"It does seem strange," Louise agreed, leaning on her pitchfork. Then she added, "She should have gotten another foal to look after, to take her mind off Curiosity. But her dad told me she refused point-blank to have another pony."

"Well, I suppose she still loves Curiosity too much," Mandy said thoughtfully. She finished brushing Montana and started putting the brushes back into the plastic grooming kit.

"You've done a great job on Montana." Louise emerged from the stable and looked approvingly at the pony's smooth and glossy coat. Then she waved at her dad, who was standing at the gate.

"Do you girls want to come along to Sittaford Farm?" he called. "Some of Peter Taylor's sheep are loose on the moor. Adam and I are going to help."

Louise looked at Mandy, who nodded eagerly. "Give us five minutes," Louise called. "We'll turn the ponies out into the field first, okay?"

"Right," Mark said. "We'll be waiting in the truck."

Mark drove his truck as fast as the gravel road would allow. Mandy felt every lurch and jolt in muscles that were tender from all the riding she had done. She held on tight in the open back of the pickup, her fair hair flying around her face. Beside her, Louise grinned with delight as they careered along.

They drove across the moor, following a long line of wire mesh fencing, until they arrived at a place where the wire was crumpled and trodden into the soft soil.

"Look at that!" Mandy heard Mark exclaim from the driver's seat. He braked sharply. "A whole section is down. This must be where the sheep escaped." He and Dr. Adam got out and looked around, shading their eyes from the glare of the sun. They could see Peter Taylor on the hillside, waving his arms.

"He's calling us," Mark said. "Come on."

Mandy and Louise jumped from the back of the truck and raced down the hill toward Abby's dad. As Mandy drew closer, she could see that Mr. Taylor was kneeling over a large white shape that twitched and wriggled in his arms. He appeared to be struggling with one of the sheep.

"Dad!" Mandy called. She was out of breath from her spring downhill. Dr. Adam was still way behind. "Hurry," Mandy urged him. "I think Mr. Taylor has a problem with one of the sheep."

Dr. Adam gave Mandy the thumbs-up sign and began to run. "Good thing I've got this, then, isn't it?" He grinned, drawing alongside her and holding up the compact little case that held all of his emergency veterinary supplies.

"Great," Mandy agreed, and ran on down the hill.

"Hello, Mark." Mr. Taylor stood up to greet Mark, then shook hands with Dr. Adam.

"Adam is a vet, which is handy," Mark said. "It looks like you're going to need help here."

"Oh! Poor thing!" Mandy said, frowning worriedly at the distressed sheep. It looked as though the animal had been struggling for hours in some old barbed wire. The sharp, rusted barbs were coiled tightly around her forelegs, and her wool was stained with blood. She was panting hard with fear, and her sides heaved.

"I'm really glad you're here, Adam," said Mr. Taylor. "I found this ewe while I was rounding up the other sheep. Goodness knows how she managed to get so tangled up in this barbed wire — and she's about to lamb, too."

"I'll take a look," Dr. Adam said. "It appears pretty nasty. Easy, girl," he said soothingly as he got down on his knees. "Don't struggle now. It'll only make things much worse."

The imprisoned sheep fought to pull free, which made the wire tear at her leg.

"Oh, no," Louise murmured, watching helplessly beside Mandy.

"Any idea how many of your sheep have escaped, Peter?" asked Mark.

"Not too many, five or six," the farmer answered. "I'll round them up, no problem, when this is taken care of."

"I'll give you a hand mending that break in the fence," Mark offered.

"Thanks," said Mr. Taylor. "I'm short on help this week while Dan is away."

"Go ahead," Dr. Adam advised. "Get the other sheep back up to the field. I'll be fine here with the ewe for a few minutes. I'll have to examine her, and then we'll need to get her back to the farm."

"All right. We won't be long," Peter Taylor said, sounding relieved. "We'll drive back to pick you up."

"Sure." Dr. Adam nodded as the two men went after the straying sheep, who were huddled beside a narrow stream farther down the hill.

"Can I help, Dad?" Mandy asked, kneeling beside her father. She reached out and petted the sheep's bony forehead.

"Not at the moment, thanks, love," her dad answered. He carefully examined the ewe's bleeding forelegs, holding one of them firmly as she tried to pull away.

"Can't you give her something to help her to relax or

something?" Louise asked. "She doesn't seem to like what you're doing to her!"

"I can't sedate her when she is so close to having her lamb," Dr. Adam explained. "She doesn't have long to go now."

Trying to ignore the ewe's pitiful bleating, Mandy and Louise helped Dr. Adam unravel the wire. Mandy gave a sigh of relief when at last the sheep was free of the rusty coil.

"Here come Peter and Mark with the truck," Dr. Adam said grimly. "We'll take the wire back to the farm and dispose of it safely. Thanks, both of you."

Mandy held tight to the sheep's thick fleece, but the animal showed no desire to run away this time, not even when Peter's truck pulled up. Mandy noticed with a sinking feeling that the back wheel was as flat as a pancake.

"That's *just* what we need!" Peter said in annoyance, getting out and slamming the door hard. "A puncture."

"Ah," said Dr. Adam wearily. "Yes, that's a nuisance. Do you have a spare?"

"Yes. It'll only take a moment to change," Peter Taylor said. "Can you hang onto her for a bit longer?"

"She's exhausted," Dr. Adam said. "She's not going anywhere now."

Mandy straightened up and stretched. Her back was sore from bending over the ewe.

"I'll be fine here, love," Dr. Adam said gently. "You've been a great help, but you don't need to hold onto her now. Mark and Peter will be able to get her onto the truck."

"Okay," said Mandy, giving the ewe one last pat. She turned to Louise who was watching the sheep from a little way off. "Maybe we can go riding this afternoon, Lou? We'll ask Abby to go with us. After all, that's what her mom wanted."

"Hmm," said Lou, making a face. "We'll ask, but I wouldn't count on her coming along." Then she gave a gasp. "Look, Mandy! Ponies! Over there!" Louise's face lit up with pleasure. She grabbed Mandy's shoulder and pointed across the stream to a herd of shaggy ponies, standing knee-deep in the heather. "See them?" Louise hurried toward the stream, dragging Mandy with her. "Come on!"

"Don't go too far!" Dr. Adam called. "We'll be leaving as soon as Mr. Taylor replaces that tire."

"Okay, Dad," said Mandy. "Are they really wild?" she asked Louise excitedly, her eyes fixed on the cluster of sturdy ponies.

"Not exactly," Louise told her. "They're mares who belong to the farmers here. They have them covered by a stallion, then turn them loose onto the open moor until they are ready to foal. Aren't they great?"

"Oh, yes," Mandy agreed. "But there isn't much for them to eat here, is there?" She looked out across the barren, rocky moorland and thought of the bulging hay nets and alfafa treats for the ponies back at Whitehorse Farm.

"Oh, they're tough," Louise said admiringly as they walked a little closer to the herd. "They're used to surviving on not much grass."

The ponies drowsed or grazed peacefully, cropping at the short grass and flicking away the flies with their tails.

"She's a beauty," Louise said, pointing out a bay pony with a very long black tail and mane. The pony lifted her head and looked across at Louise and Mandy. Then she kicked up her heels, wheeled around, and went flying off across the moor.

"Uh-oh, I spooked her," Louise said. She stared after the pony, watching it intently as it raced around. "Isn't she wonderful!"

Mandy looked back at the herd. They had started to move off, made uneasy by the bay mare's nervousness. Their ears were forward, and they jostled one another in their haste to move away from the intruders.

"Oh, don't go," said Mandy softly, willing the ponies to stay. But the group broke up and cantered off toward the bay pony. "What a shame," Mandy began, then she stopped. Her heart did a somersault, and she bit down on her lip to stop herself from shouting out.

One pony had stayed behind — a skewbald foal. It stood and looked directly at Mandy, who kept statue still, her heart hammering. It looked exactly like the one she had seen in the fog the day before yesterday. Its face had the same distinctive white stripe. It stood in the heather, gazing steadily at Mandy. Mesmerized, Mandy stared back at it.

"They've gone," said Louise, who had wandered back to Mandy's side. "I really love —"

"Shh!" Mandy pleaded, then added in a whisper, "Keep still. Lou, *look*!"

"What?" Louise asked, following the direction of Mandy's gaze. "What *is* it?"

"It's a skewbald foal — *there*, do you see it?" Mandy grabbed her cousin's T-shirt in her urgency.

"No . . . what foal?" Louise shaded her eyes and peered where Mandy pointed.

The foal looked back at them. Not daring to take a step forward, Mandy narrowed her eyes and tried to focus in the bright sunlight. But the image she had seen so clearly seconds before had begun to fade. It was growing fainter by the second. Mandy rubbed her eyes, and when she next looked up, the foal had gone.

"Never mind," said Mandy, letting go of Louise's sleeve. "It's gone now." She felt dizzy and disoriented. *It must be the sun*, she thought.

"Well, I didn't see anything. Are you sure? A foal? All on its own? Why didn't it go with the rest of the herd?" Louise sounded skeptical.

"I don't know," Mandy answered softly. "It was just . . . there."

"Come on, my dad's waving to us," Louise said, looking up the hill. She started off toward the truck. "Let's go."

Mandy trailed behind her cousin. It had been the same foal as the one in the fog, she was sure of it! Why hadn't Louise been able to see it? And where had it gone?

"Mandy!" her father yelled. "Hurry up!"

Even from this distance, Mandy could see the ewe lying in the back of Mr. Taylor's pickup. Dr. Adam was having a hard time holding onto it as it struggled to get out of the unfamiliar truck.

Mandy began to run, hoping desperately that the sheep and her unborn lamb would be all right. But as she neared the top of the hill, she paused and looked back down to the river. All was still and quiet, and the ponies had gone, including the skewbald foal. Mandy had seen it so clearly. So why hadn't Louise seen it, too?

Six

"Slowpoke!" Louise teased as Mandy scrambled aboard the back of the truck.

"Sorry," said Mandy, sitting down beside Lou. She was out of breath and hung onto the side of the truck as Mr. Taylor started up the hill.

The four-wheel drive climbed steadily up to the broken fence and joined the road leading back to Sittaford Farm. Mark hopped out when they reached his truck and followed them back to the farm. The yellow eyes of the ewe stared balefully at Mandy, her nostrils flaring with every breath. She struggled a bit as the truck bounced along, but Dr. Adam held her firmly. Blood oozed from a gash on her leg.

Mandy immediately forgot about the skewbald foal and leaned over to brush the flies off the ewe's ears. "Will you have to stitch that?" she asked her dad, pointing to the wound.

"Yes." He nodded. "It's a mess, isn't it?"

It wasn't long before the truck came to a lurching halt outside the barn at Sittaford Farm.

"Easy, Peter!" called Dr. Adam. "We don't want this ewe lambing in the back of the truck."

Louise jumped down from the back. "I'm starving," she announced.

"You girls go on up to the house, if you want," Mr. Taylor suggested as he unfastened the flaps at the rear of the vehicle. "My wife might have a sandwich for you."

But Mandy shook her head. "I'll stay for a while," she said. She was hungry, too, but she wanted to see the ewe made comfortable.

"Catch you later, then," said Lou. "My stomach won't wait any longer."

With Mark and Mr. Taylor's help, Dr. Adam carried the ewe to a straw-filled stall in a barn and laid her down. She grunted heavily and tried to get to her feet. But Peter Taylor held her down while Dr. Adam took a syringe out of his bag and filled it with a liquid antibiotic. After he'd injected the sheep, he carefully cleaned the area around the wound with an antiseptic wash. He injected her again, this time with a local anesthetic into the skin around the wound. As soon as it had taken effect, he neatly stitched the jagged gash.

Adam Hope had just cut the knot of the final stitch when the ewe began to pant and her sides rippled with strong spasms.

"Uh-oh," he said. "We were just in time. I think she's going to lamb."

"Oh, wow," Mandy said. She loved watching animals give birth.

The ewe struggled to her feet, panting hard, then lay down again. She turned around and looked at her stomach. She was bleating and straining. It wasn't long before Dr. Adam was putting on his gloves to examine her.

"What's wrong, Dad?" Mandy whispered. She could tell things were not going well.

"She's pretty exhausted from her ordeal," Dr. Adam explained. "She can't find the strength she needs right now."

The minutes ticked by while Mandy and the three men watched the ewe struggle to have her lamb. It was hot in the stall, and Mandy's concern for the sheep was growing.

"She's not having any success," Dr. Adam announced finally. "I'm going to help her out with a hormone injection. That'll get things moving."

Mandy slipped out to get some fresh straw to spread around the stall. She wanted to make it as comfortable as possible for the arrival of the lamb. When the bed was ready, she sat on her haunches at the edge of the stall and waited. At last, the weary ewe gave one last heave, and a tiny lamb slithered damply onto the straw.

"Oh, thank goodness!" said Mandy, gazing at it in delight. "It's so tiny!"

The sheep showed no interest in licking her baby clean, so Dr. Adam passed Mandy a small towel. She knew what to do. As she lifted it gently, she marveled at how light and fragile it was. She buffed the lamb softly, and it whimpered and flopped in her arms.

The ewe began to pant and strain again. Dr. Adam looked surprised. "It looks like she's going to have another one!"

Sure enough, a second tiny lamb soon tumbled onto the straw.

"Oh, Dad, they're lovely!" said Mandy. "Perfect twin lambs!"

"Well done, Adam," Peter Taylor said with a grin. "I'm glad you were here. I don't think she could have done it on her own."

Adam Hope smiled. The ewe was lying in the straw, straining to sniff at her babies. Mandy's dad placed the lambs close to their mother, and immediately they began snuffling around on their bent knees, looking for milk.

"She should be fine, now," Dr. Adam said. He stood up. His knees were muddy, and his shirt was torn from where he had grappled with the barbed wire. Mandy reached up and plucked a piece of straw out of his beard.

"Thanks again, Adam," said Mr. Taylor, smiling down at the little family.

"Now, did someone say something about food?" Mandy's dad asked hopefully as he wiped his hands clean.

As she pushed open the kitchen door, Mandy was relieved to see a large oval platter of sandwiches on the table. She had just now realized how hungry she was. Abby's mother greeted her with a broad smile. "Hello, Mandy. Help yourself. Everyone else has," she said pleasantly. "Tracy's brought your mom as well, so we've got a full house. Oh, you'll want to wash your hands first."

"How's the ewe?" Louise asked.

Mandy went over to the kitchen sink and squirted liquid soap into her palms. "She's fine now — and she had twin lambs!" she announced triumphantly.

"Great!" Louise mumbled, her cheeks bulging.

"Oh, wonderful!" said Tracy Brown, smoothing Coco's soft head with her hand. The black Labrador was sitting beside her chair, eyeing her plate hopefully.

"Thank heavens you could get her back to the barn before she tried to have them when she was tangled up in that wire," Dr. Emily said. "Where's your dad now, Mandy?"

"He's on his way back with Mr. Taylor and Mark," she replied, adding, "they're all starving."

"Hmm, in that case, I'd better make some more sandwiches." Mrs. Taylor laughed.

Dr. Emily stood up and started to make a fresh pot of tea while Tracy reached across for a knife and began buttering some more scones. Abby was sitting in her usual place, beside the kitchen window. She looked up and gave Mandy a small smile, but she made no comment about the ewe.

"Did you finish your homework?" Mandy asked her.

"No," Abby said. "Not yet."

"Oh," said Mandy, not sure what else she could say to draw Abby out. She helped herself to a cheese sandwich.

"Mom, Mandy and I saw a herd of ponies on the moor

this morning!" Louise said. "There was a gorgeous bay with them."

"They must belong to Ray Cooney," Tracy said thoughtfully. "They'll be ready to foal soon, I think."

"And Mandy thought that she saw a foal," Louise went on.

Abby turned quickly away from the window. She frowned in Mandy's direction.

"But I *did* see a foal," Mandy reasoned, looking steadily at her cousin. "A skewbald, not that young, but less than a year, I'd say."

"Well, I couldn't see it." Louise shook her head. "Sorry, Mandy, I'm not laughing at you, honestly I'm not."

"That's okay." Mandy smiled and added, "But have you thought about getting your eyes tested?" She grinned and Louise laughed with her. Then they heard Abby give a loud gasp. The room fell silent as everyone turned to look at her.

"What is it, Abby?" her mother asked gently.

But Abby was on her feet and out the kitchen door in a flash. Her half-eaten sandwich fell to the floor as she took flight, and Coco, who had given up on Tracy and was lying underneath the table on the cool flagstone floor, made a grab for it.

"Well!" said Mrs. Taylor in a bewildered voice. "I give up with that girl!"

"What on earth's got into her?" Tracy asked, frowning at the doorway.

"I'll go after her," Mandy volunteered quickly. She put her sandwich back on her plate and scraped back her chair.

"Yes, please do, Mandy." Mrs. Taylor sighed. "None of us has been able to get anywhere with her. Perhaps you'll have better luck!"

By the time Mandy came around the corner of the house, there was no sign of Abby. She stood looking around her, feeling a little frustrated. There were hundreds of acres of farmland, plus the yard, which was edged with outbuildings. Abby could have hidden just about anywhere.

She felt a warm, wet nose pushing at the palm of her hand and saw that Coco had followed her out. The Labrador's tail wagged happily, and his brown eyes shone up at Mandy.

"Where's Abby?" she asked the dog, her hands on her hips. Coco obligingly put his nose to the ground and set off across the yard. He seemed to have picked up a familiar scent.

"Oh, good Coco!" Mandy hurried after the dog. "Find Abby!" She followed the dog trustingly, but Coco soon lost interest in the trail and flopped down in the shade of the barn, his tongue lolling. As she paused, Mandy heard the faint sound of someone sniffling. She popped her head into the shadowy barn and traced the noise to a stall next door to the pen in which the injured mother ewe was lying.

Abby was leaning on the dividing partition, her chin resting on her forearms. Tears flowed freely down her cheeks as she looked down at the sheep and her lambs.

"I'm sure they're going to be okay," Mandy said quietly.

Abby jumped. "Oh! You frightened me!" she said. Angrily, she wiped away her tears.

"I'm sorry," said Mandy. "I didn't mean to sneak up on you. It's just that you seemed so upset. I thought you might be worried about the sheep."

"Well, I'm fine," Abby retorted, hiding her face in her arms. "And so is the sheep, no thanks to me."

"What's the matter, Abby?" Mandy persisted. "What's making you so sad?"

Abby sniffed, then turned and walked to the gate of the stall, clenching her hands over the top bar. "Look," she said to Mandy, who had followed her, "it's nice of you to care about me, especially since you don't even know me. But I'm okay, really I am."

"Louise told me about Curiosity," Mandy said. "It must have broken your heart when she died."

Abby's head flew up and she looked straight at Mandy. "Yes, well," she said, after a few seconds. "It was my own stupid fault, so I have to live with the consequences."

"Don't be so hard on yourself," Mandy said.

Abby lapsed into silence. She began to examine her bitten nails. Mandy felt helpless. There seemed no way to break through the wall poor Abby had built around herself. She gave a big sigh and looked out the door of the barn across the stretch of moorland bordering

Sittaford Farm. A flock of grackles wheeled about in the sky, cawing noisily. Sturdy post-and-nail fencing separated the yard from the open countryside.

When the skewbald foal suddenly appeared at the fence, Mandy was at first too surprised to move or think. She watched it for a second, blinked several times, then looked at it again. It was still there, gazing searchingly at her with its huge dark eyes. It looked calmly at her, as if it trusted her to know what to do. Mandy glanced at Abby, who was still studying her fingernails.

"Look," Mandy said quietly, touching Abby's shoulder. "Do you know who owns that sweet pony? I've seen it before, you know."

Abby pulled away from Mandy's touch and looked in the direction Mandy was pointing. Then she gasped, and her hands flew up to her mouth. "Go away!" she shouted wildly, and flapped her arms frantically at the foal. "Leave me alone, please. Go away!"

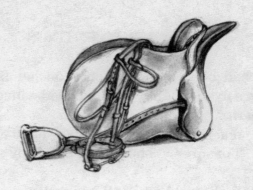

Seven

It was the very last reaction Mandy had expected from Abby. Her face had gone chalk white as she shouted at the foal. But it had no effect. The skewbald stood her ground. Her ears twitched as she listened to Abby's cries, but her soft eyes seemed never to leave Abby's face.

"Hush!" Mandy pleaded in a whisper. "Please, Abby — there's no need." She couldn't take her eyes off the little skewbald. Her coat wasn't rough and muddy like the other ponies Mandy had seen on the moor. Her chestnut legs and darker head were glossy, and her forelock and mane became whiter as it grew down toward her withers. She had big, creamy patches on her flanks. The brown eyes fixed on Abby seemed filled with gentleness and concern.

Mandy reached out and put her hand on Abby's shoulder. "I'm sure —" she began, but Abby spun away from her.

"No! No!" she sobbed. "Tell her to leave me alone!" Abby took to her heels, flying around the corner of the barn, her blond ponytail bobbing.

Mandy chased after her, all the way back up to the house. As she ran, she puzzled over Abby's bizarre reaction.

Abby flung open the front door of the house, Mandy hot on her heels. Avoiding the kitchen, where lunch was still in progress, she raced up the stairs and into her bedroom. Breathing hard, she flung herself onto her bed, then burst into fresh tears.

"What's the matter?" Mandy begged, coming to a halt in the doorway. "Please tell me!"

Abby snatched a tissue from a box on her desk and blew her nose noisily, then dried her face. As she gazed at Mandy, puzzlement flooded her face. "You can *see* her!" she gasped.

"Yes, I can," Mandy answered softly. "Isn't she wonderful?" Her eyes shone.

"But *how*?" Abby asked her. "I mean, how can you? Nobody else can see her."

"What do you mean?" Mandy frowned.

"Curiosity!" Abby wailed, covering her eyes with her trembling hands. "No one has noticed her, not once since she appeared."

Mandy felt her heart lurch. Curiosity? Abby's dead foal? Was Abby saying that they'd just seen a ghost?

Suddenly, everything seemed to click into place for Mandy. It would explain why there was something so different, so ghostly about the foal and why no one else could see her. "But Abby, that's wonderful!" said Mandy.

"Wonderful? No!" Abby shook her head, her expression fearful. "Don't you see? She's coming back to haunt me. You don't understand. She wants to hurt me. It's probably her fault that those sheep got out."

"But that's absurd. The fence was broken — I saw it." Mandy frowned. She came into the room and sat down on Abby's bed. "And why would Curiosity want to make trouble for you?"

"Because of what I did," Abby said miserably, sitting beside Mandy. "I — I *killed* her!"

"Abby," said Mandy, in her gentlest voice. "It was an accident. It wasn't anybody's fault."

"But if I hadn't asked my dad to change the radio station in the car, he wouldn't have taken his eyes off the road." Abby put her hands over her eyes, as though she was trying to stop herself from remembering that terrible day. "She's angry."

"Oh, Abby, no! You mustn't think that!" Mandy begged.

"I've seen her on the moor," Abby continued quietly. Her eyes had narrowed, and the fearful expression had returned to her face. "Several times now. At first, I thought I was imagining it."

"Yes." Mandy nodded. She knew what that felt like. "Did you tell anyone about her? Your mom or your dad?"

Abby shook her head, frowning. "I don't want anyone to laugh at me," she said. "And I'm sure no one else has seen her. Mom and Dad have been great, but they think I should forget about Curiosity and get on with my life. But I can't!"

"I know," Mandy said calmly. "It must be really hard for you."

Abby pulled the pillow on her bed to her chest and hugged it. Her face was crumpled with unhappiness. She began speaking in a low voice. "Curiosity meant the world to me. From the time she arrived at the farm when she was six months old, she and I were practically never apart."

"Go on," Mandy said quietly. Her heart thudded in her chest, and her mind was whirling with a thousand questions, but she knew it was important to listen to what Abby had to say.

"She was all mine," Abby said fiercely, remembering. "She followed me around like a puppy. I always had someone to be with, to talk to and have fun with."

"A real friend," Mandy agreed, remembering that Abby was an only child. Mandy didn't have any brothers or sisters, either, but at least she lived in a busy village, and her best friend, James Hunter, lived just down the road.

"And then Curiosity got sick when she was about ten months old. Our vet was away on vacation, so Dad suggested we drive over to Murchington to see a friend of his who's a vet. That was when it happened." Abby stopped and clutched her pillow. A single tear ran down her cheek.

"How soon after the accident did you see her?" Mandy asked softly, her arm around Abby's shoulders.

Abby gave a shudder. "I was in my bedroom, the night before spring break. It was pretty late, but I couldn't sleep. I heard a rustling sound and went to the window to look out. I thought it might be our cat trying to find a way in. I saw Curiosity standing in the garden. For a split second, I thought she was real. I wanted so badly to believe that she was alive — that she'd come back to me!"

"Yes, of course." Mandy nodded, hugging Abby a bit harder.

"But I knew, really, in my heart, that it wasn't possible. There was a half-moon, and it was misty, and her outline seemed to shimmer — but still, it was Curiosity!"

"What did you do?" Mandy held her breath, imagining the shock and the joy of seeing the foal standing there.

"I rushed downstairs and out into the garden. It was dark, and I fell over a wheelbarrow that had been left out. When I got up again, Curiosity had gone."

"Oh!" Mandy felt desperately sorry for the unhappy girl, but she couldn't think of anything to say that might make her feel better.

Abby continued. "Of course, Mom and Dad heard the noise I made when I fell over. They came rushing out and tried to persuade me that I had been dreaming about Curiosity. But I hadn't."

"No, you hadn't." Mandy smiled encouragingly at Abby.

"For a while, I thought maybe I *had* imagined Curiosity being there. But the next day I saw her again, in a field close to the house. I raced into the field, calling her name, but I couldn't see her! I searched and searched. It was broad daylight, so I knew then that I hadn't been dreaming," Abby said. "I just don't know what to think anymore. Whenever I go outside, she's always there. And I'm really scared of her now. I just wish she'd leave!"

"Wish who'd leave?" said a voice at the door.

Mandy and Abby looked up, startled. Neither of them had heard the door open.

Louise looked in at them. "Who are you talking about?" she asked.

"Just a . . . girl at my school," Abby said quickly as Louise came in.

"Oh." Louise shrugged. "Where did you two go, anyway? I've been looking all over for you."

"We went to check on the ewe," Mandy said.

"Do you feel like riding this afternoon?" Louise asked casually. She had picked up one of Abby's horse magazines from a pile and was leafing through it.

"Yes," Mandy said immediately.

"No," said Abby. "Not me."

Mandy was disappointed. "Oh, please come, Abby," she said. "It'll be fun."

"I don't like riding anymore," Abby said. She began to bite her nails. Mandy said nothing.

"You've got to put that accident behind you," Louise urged Abby. "I mean it. Try to forget about what happened. You can't go on being sad forever!"

Mandy stood up. She knew Abby wasn't only sad, she was terribly afraid. She looked sympathetically at Abby's pale, miserable face. "We'll ride together," she suggested. "Please, Abby. I'd really love it if you came."

Abby looked steadily back at Mandy. "Well, okay," she said in a small voice. "Maybe I should."

"Huh! I like *that* — the answer's no when I ask you to come!" Louise teased as they headed downstairs. She grinned at Abby and squeezed her arm affectionately. "But I don't care *why* you're going riding, just as long as you come."

"Thank you for a delicious lunch," Dr. Emily said to Mrs. Taylor as they came into the kitchen.

"It was great to see you," Abby's mom replied. Then she turned toward the door and her face lit up. "Oh, Abby! There you are. Is everything okay?"

"Fine," Abby mumbled, sounding a little shy. "Sorry I rushed out like that."

"Mark and I are going fishing this afternoon," Dr. Adam announced enthusiastically. "Do any of you want to come along?"

"No, thanks," Mandy said. "We're going for a ride." Abby's mom looked hopefully from Mandy to Louise. "And Abby's coming with us," Mandy added, grinning.

Abby's mother smiled. "Oh, *good*!" She sounded very relieved.

"We'll see you back at Whitehorse Farm later," Louise said.

"You'll watch out for bogs, won't you?" Mrs. Taylor

reminded them. At the mention of the word, Abby gave a shudder.

"We'll be very careful, Mrs. Taylor," Mandy assured her.

"Enjoy your ride." Dr. Emily gave Mandy a hug. "Tracy and I are going into Chagford to the antique market. We'll see you back at the farm around suppertime, Mandy."

"Bye, Mom," said Mandy. She turned to Abby, who was standing with her back to them, staring out the kitchen window. Mandy went over and linked arms with her. "Come on, Abby," she said with determination. "Let's go and get those ponies."

On the walk back to Whitehorse Farm, Mandy tried to keep Abby's spirits up by telling her stories about her life in Welford. "I've met some really unusual animals," she said. "Every day is a surprise at Animal Ark."

Although Abby smiled wanly at her, Mandy could tell by glancing sideways at her face that she wasn't really listening. Abby's eyes darted nervously from side to side, scouring the moors that stretched away on either side of them. Louise didn't seem to notice, but Mandy could tell Abby was on the lookout for Curiosity.

As they approached the field where the Whitehorse Farm ponies grazed, they could hear them, eagerly pulling at the spring grass. They entered the yard and went straight to the tack room to collect saddles and bridles.

Louise saddled up Fern, and Mandy chose to ride Cinders again. Abby settled for Pecan.

"She can be a bit slow," Louise told her hesitantly. "You'd be better with Montana or —"

"She'll be fine, thanks," Abby said quietly, lowering a saddle onto the pony's broad roan back.

Louise led the way out to where the moor began to dip down a valley toward the meandering river. She pushed Fern into a canter and then a full gallop, but Mandy lagged behind, keeping Abby company. Abby seemed fairly cheerful as she told Mandy about a necklace she'd been given by her grandmother recently.

"Isn't it pretty out here?" said Mandy, waving her arm around at the endless green moorland.

"Well, I haven't seen — you know who. Have you?" Abby replied, lowering her voice.

"No, not today," Mandy admitted. "But I don't think I'd mind if I did."

Abby looked anxious and preoccupied as Louise circled back to join them.

"Fern needs a really good run, so I'm going on up to Scorhill Stone Circle," she said breathlessly. "I'll meet you there, okay?"

"Do you know the way there, Abby?" asked Mandy. Abby nodded.

"Pecan *will* go faster than a walk, you know!" Louise chuckled as she sped away.

Looking stung, Abby immediately spurred Pecan into a brisk trot. Mandy rode beside her until the brooding stones of the great circle lay directly ahead of them, casting pointed shadows in the afternoon sunlight. They reined the ponies in and dismounted at the top of the hill, which sloped down to the circle of stones. A flock of skylarks dipped and swooped above them, calling shrilly to one another.

"Wow," Mandy breathed. "This place is really amazing!"

"Where's Louise?" said Abby, looking around.

Mandy glanced down at the stone circle. Light from the late afternoon sun had turned the jagged tips of the stones a fiery gold. Mandy's eyes were drawn to the center of the ring where, somehow, the light seemed to be most intense. It shimmered and danced, as if it was held there by the stones. Mandy blinked in amazement. It was as though the force of the sun had been collected in this ancient and magical place, radiating outward in a blaze of light.

And then Mandy felt her heart start to beat faster. There, in the heart of the circle, stood Curiosity.

There was no mistaking the skewbald foal. Her little ears were pricked, and the same kind, concerned look was on her face. Mandy turned to Abby excitedly. She hoped to prove to her new friend once and for all that the foal was not appearing to them because she was angry with Abby. "Abby! Look! Curiosity is here," she whispered.

Abby was just swinging her leg over Pecan's back. She sat down hard in the saddle and snatched up the reins. Her knuckles turned white as she gripped the leather fiercely.

"No! Oh, no!" she wailed, turning Pecan away from the circle of stones. "Come on, Mandy, let's go, please."

"Abby —" Mandy began, but she didn't finish her sentence. Pecan suddenly threw back his head and reared up. Mandy was astonished. Pecan was usually very docile, yet he was staggering backward on his hind legs in obvious terror.

Abby was taken by surprise. She flew backward out of the saddle and landed heavily on her side in a patch of heather. For a moment she lay there, stunned. As Mandy rushed over to help her to her feet, she saw a light brown snake slithering away under a nearby rock. "Are you hurt, Abby?" She gently pulled Abby up off the ground.

"I hurt my hip," she gasped, then she turned on

Mandy, tears flowing hotly down her cheeks. "What did I tell you? Curiosity scared Pecan! The slowest pony at Whitehorse Farm, and even he's scared!"

"It was a snake," Mandy said softly. "I saw it. Pecan was startled by a snake." But from the look on Abby's face, Mandy could tell that she didn't believe her. "Well, you wait here, then," she told Abby. "I'm going into the circle. I want to see how close I can get to Curiosity."

Eight

Mandy tied Cinders's reins securely to a tall clump of heather. The patient brown mare began to graze as Mandy headed down the slope toward the circle. She could see the foal clearly, standing in the middle of the stones, bathed in the unnatural, shimmering light. Mandy half expected the foal to turn and flee as she approached the stones, but Curiosity remained rooted to the spot. Mandy was more convinced than ever that the foal was communicating with her, silently willing her to come closer.

As Mandy met the foal's steady, dark gaze, she felt her

heart fluttering and her tummy churning. What if Abby was right? What if Curiosity was angry about her death? Mandy looked her straight in the eye, challenging her to show her true feelings. But what Mandy saw there was not anger or fear but concern. Curiosity's brown eyes were like pools of river water. It seemed to Mandy that the foal was asking for her trust.

Walking slowly, Mandy went up to the first of the stones that guarded the mysterious circle. It was cool to the touch, in spite of being bathed in light from the sinking sun. Her tail swishing, her ears forward, the foal watched her come. Mandy knew that was a good sign. If Curiosity had her ears back, Mandy doubted she would have the courage not to turn and run. She took another step toward the heart of the circle, where Curiosity stood so still.

"Hello," Mandy said in her softest voice. "Hello, little Curiosity." She held out her hand. Though she could clearly see the foal, she seemed too far away to touch.

"Mandy! Mandy!" She could hear Abby calling her back, her voice urgent and afraid. "Please come back."

Mandy raised her hand and waved it high above her head to signal to Abby that she was fine. She didn't want to risk frightening the foal by calling out to Abby.

Standing there, bathed in the soft golden light of the

circle, with only the foal for company, Mandy felt the moor slide away from her. It seemed to fade and disappear into an enveloping mist. She felt a peculiar sensation, as though she was being held still by an unseen force. It was suddenly quiet. Even the birds had stopped singing. But Mandy felt quite calm. "Come," she murmured. "Come, Curiosity."

But the foal continued to stand just out of her reach. Mandy took a step closer, reaching out to pat the sweet little face. Curiosity tossed her mane and swished her tail. Mandy thought she heard a faint, friendly nicker, but she couldn't be sure. Although Mandy had lost count of all the animals she had helped, this time she had the strangest feeling that Curiosity wanted to help her. But how?

Suddenly, the mood in the circle changed abruptly. The quiet was shattered by the harsh sound of a pony's distant neighing. Again and again, louder and louder, Mandy heard the squealing sound. Somewhere there was a pony in terrible distress! It seemed to be coming from beyond where Curiosity stood. She stood rooted to the spot, trying to identify the source of the pitiful calling. The big stones stood silently all around her, like cold, unfeeling guards.

Mandy looked back toward where she'd left Abby,

her heart pounding. When she turned back, Curiosity
was gone.

"Abby! Pecan!" Mandy shouted, turning and running
out of the circle. She stumbled back up the hill. Dusk
had turned the moor a soft rose color, and the sky was
streaked with red and orange where the sun was going
down. The skylarks wheeled about, chirping and calling. At the top of the hill, Abby sat astride Pecan, a look
of alarm on her face. "Mandy! Are you all right?" she
asked.

"I'm fine," Mandy answered. "Are you? And Pecan?"

"Yes, we're okay. Why?" Abby looked puzzled.

"Oh, no reason." In that instant, Mandy decided not to
say anything to Abby about the pony she'd heard in the
circle. Hearing the shriek of a pony she couldn't see had
been one of the most terrifying things she had ever ex-
perienced. She couldn't have imagined it, she knew she
couldn't. The sound had given her goose bumps, and
she still felt a chill creeping up her spine. Mandy gave
herself a shake and started to untie Cinders, who was
cropping the short grass under the heather.

"I was worried about you," Abby said as Mandy
swung herself up into the saddle. "Did you see her? Curiosity, I mean?"

"Clearly," Mandy said. She pictured again the foal's

gentle, pleading face. "You know, I don't think she wants to hurt you at all. She seems — I don't know, concerned, as if she wants to help you in some way."

"*Help me?*" echoed Abby in disbelief as the ponies began to walk side by side away from Scorhill Stone Circle.

"Yes." Mandy was firm. "I sensed it really strongly. But I don't know how, exactly."

"Well, don't trust her," Abby said. "My hip is really sore, and poor Pecan got the fright of his life."

"I'm sorry, Abby," Mandy said reasonably. "But I honestly believe that if Curiosity was here because she was angry — if she wanted to do you harm — then the signs would be more obvious! It's all been coincidence up to now. I mean, you've never actually *seen* the foal doing anything to hurt you."

"I wonder where Louise has gone?" said Abby, changing the subject.

"She might have decided to go home," said Mandy. "The sun's nearly gone down. It'll be dark soon."

The girls fell silent. Mandy had a lot on her mind. Curiosity was trying to tell them something, of that she was certain.

"Look! There's Lou!" cried Abby suddenly.

Louise came charging across the moor toward them. Her cheeks were flushed pink from her exertion. Fern's coat was dark with sweat after her canter. She had flecks of foam around her lips, and her nostrils were flaring.

"We've had the most fabulous ride!" Louise gasped. "Did you two have a nice afternoon?"

"You said you'd meet us at the circle," Abby said accusingly.

"Well." Louise grinned at them. "I changed my mind. Fern and I went to the river instead." She fell into step beside Pecan, walking shoulder to shoulder with Abby. The ponies walked three abreast, and Fern seemed pleased to have slowed down.

"Abby fell off," Mandy told Louise. "Pecan was scared by a snake."

"Oh!" Louise was instantly concerned. "Are you okay?"

"Fine," Abby said. "I just bumped my hip."

"It's your birthday next week," Louise remembered suddenly. "Are you — maybe — going to ask your parents for another pony?"

"No," Abby said. "I don't think so."

"How old will you be?" Mandy asked. She had to pull sharply on the reins, because Cinders had stopped for a snack.

"Thirteen," Abby said. "I'm getting a computer. That's what I want."

"Great! Lucky you," Mandy answered.

Abby smiled at Mandy. "I told you about the locket my grandma sent me, didn't I? She lives in London. It's real gold! It has a picture of her in it."

"It sounds gorgeous," Louise said.

"Take a look, if you like. I'm wearing it," Abby said.

Mandy and Louise both turned to see the locket as Abby fumbled at her neck. She felt inside her T-shirt and prodded at her collarbone. "Oh, no!" she cried. "It's not there! I've lost it."

Mandy reined Cinders to a halt. "Are you sure you had it on?" she asked.

"Yes!" Abby was fighting back tears. "I put it on the moment it arrived in the mail. It was beautiful! Oh, what am I going to tell my mom? And my grandma!"

"We'll find it," Louise said. "It must be somewhere. I'll go back and see if I can spot it on the ground. The clasp might have come undone."

"Thanks, Louise!" mumbled Abby miserably, patting her T-shirt and feeling in the pockets of her jodhpurs in case the necklace had slipped off into her clothes.

The moment Louise cantered off, Abby turned to Mandy. "See? Bad things just keep happening, and it's always when Curiosity is around!"

Mandy turned in her saddle to look back at Louise. She was bending down in her saddle, peering at the ground. It was safe to talk.

"But if you'd been close enough to look at her face," Mandy pleaded, "you'd know she wasn't angry. Her eyes are full of warmth and kindness."

"Shhh!" Abby hissed. "Louise is coming back."

"There's no sign of any necklace," Louise reported, trotting up to them. "Not that I can see. I'm so sorry, Abby. Shall we go back to Scorhill Circle to look? Maybe you dropped it there?"

"No!" Abby said quickly, almost shouting. "I mean, I'm sure I didn't."

"Okay," Louise said. She glanced at Mandy, her eyebrows raised.

Tears began to slide down Abby's cheeks. She dashed them away impatiently with the back of her hand. "Oh, well," she said, "I'd better get back and face my mom. She's going to be furious."

The ponies walked slowly and sadly across the last stretch of the moor and along the lane to the stables at Whitehorse Farm. They broke into a trot as the yard came into sight, eager for a rest and their food.

Mandy felt very troubled. She had hoped that she would be able to help Abby, but it seemed she had only made things worse. She had failed to persuade her that Curiosity meant her no harm. There seemed nothing else she could do.

*   *   *

When they'd given the ponies buckets of clean water and checked their hay nets, Abby got ready to go.

"I'll walk with you, if you like," Mandy offered. "I'll help explain to your mom."

"No, thanks," Abby said. "I'm fine alone. I'll see you."

Mandy and Louise watched her go. She looked lonely walking up the lane, her head hanging.

"Poor Abby!" sighed Mandy.

"Oh, don't worry!" Louise said cheerfully. "Her mom's not going to eat her alive. It was an accident. She'll understand."

But Mandy wasn't thinking about Abby's missing locket. She was thinking about her fear of Curiosity and the fact that she seemed unable to put the whole miserable business of the foal's death behind her.

Lying in bed that night, Mandy couldn't stop thinking about the fact that Curiosity kept appearing to Abby. *Why?* That was the question. Why wasn't the foal at peace? She tossed and turned so that Louise finally opened one sleepy eye.

"Mandy!" she hissed. "You're keeping me awake."

"Sorry," Mandy mumbled. She tried to lie still, but her eyes were still wide open. She couldn't forget the terrified neighing she had heard in the stone circle. It had appeared out of nowhere, the chilling shriek of a pony in trouble, echoing again and again around the circle of stones. Then it had stopped. Where had it come from, and what did it mean? Mandy shivered and pulled her quilt up under her chin. She hugged her knees. A pony was in trouble on the moor, but did it have anything to do with Curiosity?

Nine

Mandy had finally fallen asleep very late. Her dreams were filled with images of a foal dancing across the moor. He was always just out of her reach, close enough to feel his warm breath on her face yet too far away to touch.

For once, she woke up before Louise did. She slipped quietly out of bed and went downstairs without disturbing her cousin.

"Hello, love," Dr. Adam said as she appeared in the kitchen. Mandy's mom was making a pot of tea, and Mandy went over and gave her a hug.

Dr. Adam nodded in the direction of the window. "The weather's gotten worse, I'm afraid."

Mandy looked. It was cloudy, and a light rain was falling. "Oh, well," she said. "We've had lots of hot days, so we can't complain."

"You're right, it's been beautiful," Dr. Emily said.

"Morning, Mandy," said Tracy, wiping her shoes vigorously on the mat at the back door. She was carrying a plastic tub holding several warm brown eggs. "Is Louise up yet?"

Mandy smiled. "I beat her to it, for a change," she said.

"Are you game for some letterboxing today?" Tracy asked, putting the eggs on a counter and slicing into a plump loaf of brown bread.

"Letterboxing?" Mandy frowned. "What's that?"

"Aha!" Tracy exclaimed, her eyes gleaming. "It's an old tradition around these parts. It's great fun."

"It's like a giant treasure hunt over the whole moor," explained Mandy's dad.

"That's right." Tracy handed Mandy a pot of homemade jam for the table. "It started in Victorian times. A young man left his card in a bottle beside Cranmere Pool. He was hoping the lady he loved would find it, and she did. People began to leave their visiting cards in small containers and hiding them in places across the moor."

"How romantic!" Mandy cried. "You mean, a card with their name and address on it?"

"Yes, exactly," Tracy confirmed. "People would hunt out the containers, take out the cards, and replace them with cards of their own. Then they had to find the person whose name was on the card they had taken."

"That sounds like fun," Mandy said, grinning at her mom.

Dr. Adam nodded. "It's very popular these days. Mark and I used to play years ago, but we weren't much good. Thousands of boxes are hidden across this moor apparently. Each one holds a small notebook and a unique rubber stamp to make a mark in your own record book."

"How do you win the game?" Mandy asked, her enthusiasm growing.

"You don't *win*, exactly." Mrs. Brown smiled. "There isn't a prize or anything. The challenge is to figure out the clues left in each of the boxes so you can find the next one, and the reward for your hard work is the number of different stamps you collect."

Louise came in, rubbing her short hair and yawning. "Hi, everyone," she said sleepily, and sat down at the table.

"Wow," said Mandy.

"Wow what?" Louise asked.

"Letterboxing," Mandy said.

"Oh, it's great. Do you want to try it?" Louise's face brightened. "It's sort of wet for riding today, and Fern could use a rest."

"Yes!" Mandy grinned.

"Maybe Abby will go with us," Louise went on, dolloping jam onto her bread.

"I hope so," answered Mandy. But judging by Abby's downcast mood yesterday, she didn't think she would.

"It sounds like a wonderful excuse for exploring the moor." Dr. Emily smiled at Mandy. "I wish I could come along, but I promised Tracy I'd help in the garden today."

"Yes, you did!" Tracy laughed. "But I'll let you off if you really want to go letterboxing!"

"No, I'll stay," Dr. Emily said. "Mandy and Louise will tell me all about it, I'm sure."

"Did you know, Mandy," Tracy added, "there's even a letterbox club in existence for people who've been successful in finding more than a hundred boxes? So if you work hard, you may even become a member today!"

"Wow," said Mandy again. She tried to imagine how far you would have to walk to find as many as a hundred secretly stashed containers.

They hurried through breakfast, eager to get started. Just as they were finishing the last pieces of toast, Louise's dad appeared at the back door. He wiped the rain off his face with a handkerchief.

"I'm taking Mandy letterboxing," Louise announced happily.

"It's not great weather for roaming around on the moor, Lou," he warned.

"Oh, Dad!" Louise chided him, gathering up the empty plates. "We don't care about a bit of *rain*, do we, Mandy?"

Mandy grinned and shook her head.

"Well, be careful, that's all," Mr. Brown said firmly. "You know the moors, Lou. Don't get lost."

"We won't, Dad." She stood up. "Come on, Mandy. Let's go."

After Louise and Mandy had picked out thick water-proof coats and trousers for each of them, Dr. Adam drove them to Sittaford Farm. To Mandy's surprise, Abby seemed pleased to see them.

"I found the locket," she whispered before the front door to the house was fully opened. "So I didn't have to tell my mom."

"Oh! Great!" Mandy smiled, waving as her father honked the horn and drove away. "Where was it?"

"Well, that's the strange thing. I found it in a drawer on top of an old photograph of Curiosity. And I was so sure I had put it on that morning. . . ." Abby trailed off, looking puzzled.

"Well, you'd better take better care of it from now on," Louise said, playfully wagging a finger at Abby. Then she added, "So are you coming letterboxing with us?"

Abby hesitated, but only for a moment. "Okay," she answered. "It's always fun. And it *is* almost Mandy's last day. I'll just tell my mom." Abby shot off through the house, calling for her mother. She was back shortly, shrugging on a waterproof jacket.

"We'll head for Fox Tor Mire," Louise said, tugging Abby out of the door. "Come on, let's get going!"

From Sittaford Tor, they walked south across a very bleak, open stretch of moorland. Louise explained that letterboxers had to be careful not to disturb any important landmarks on the moor, and that meant not leaving messages at any of the ancient sites such as Scorhill Stone Circle. As they walked along through the fine drizzle, Mandy glanced at Abby. She seemed in better spirits, though from time to time Mandy caught her glancing furtively behind her and guessed she was watching out for Curiosity.

"How do you know where to find the first box?" Mandy asked.

"You don't know for certain," Abby said. "You look for places where people are likely to have hidden a box, or you just have to keep an eye out for someone who might be looking, too. Look out for people who are rummaging in the undergrowth or examining a hollow tree trunk. That's always a good clue!"

They walked on, Louise slightly in the lead. It gave Mandy a chance to whisper to Abby. "You seem to be a little happier today," she remarked.

"I've been doing some thinking," Abby said in a low voice. "Maybe I am being silly thinking that Curiosity's angry."

"I think that maybe you are," Mandy agreed, feeling sad about it. She longed to see the little foal again and to try to discover the reason for her presence.

"Perhaps she's finally gone away," Abby said.

"Maybe," Mandy said, though she hoped not. She looked behind her. Clouds had begun to pack along the horizon. The air seemed to have thickened. The ground was spongy from the rain, and Mandy's shoes felt heavy with mud. Suddenly, Louise put out a hand, and Mandy walked right into it.

"Ouch," she said, startled.

"Don't go any farther!" Louise said, her hand still

pressed against Mandy's arm. "Look." She put out the toe of her running shoe and touched the earth in front of her. The ground wobbled alarmingly.

"Bog!" Abby gasped.

"It's like a big mound of Jell-O," Mandy said wonderingly. She bent down and poked at the ground with her finger. It punctured the surface, and water oozed up into a small pool around it. Mandy stood up. "Oh, yuck," she said. "I don't want to fall into that!"

"Right," Louise said in a businesslike manner. "Let's move over this way."

"Wait a minute!" Abby cried. "What's this in there?"

"What's what?" Louise asked.

Abby crouched down and peered at a large rock. It was a granite boulder almost split in two by a deep horizontal crevice. Wedged onto the narrow shelf was a small metal box.

"Oh, terrific, Abby!" Louise cried excitedly. "I think we've found our first letterbox!"

Mandy stooped beside Abby and tugged at the box. It came free with a loud scraping noise and a shower of small stones.

They gathered in a circle, and Abby eased off the tightly fitting lid, which parted from the tin with a loud pop. Inside, a sheet of paper, yellowed with age, lay folded and wrapped in layers of tissue paper. Beside it was a rubber stamp, fashioned in the shape of an eagle, its wings outstretched.

"Oh, look," breathed Mandy, thrilled. "It's a really old one."

Abby peeled off the protective covering.

Although the rain had all but stopped, Louise was cautious. "Don't let it get wet," she said, peering over Abby's shoulder as she unfolded the paper. The words of the clue had been written in black ink.

"What amazing writing," Mandy said, admiring the decorative twists and curls of each letter.

Louise began to read aloud. *"Return the box where it was found, the next one's hidden underground, beside a post upon the moor, one mile north of Sittaford Tor."*

"Sittaford Tor! That's where we've just come from," Abby said.

"What do we do now?" Mandy asked Lou, unable to tear her eyes away from the piece of paper with the spidery black writing.

Louise fumbled in her jacket pocket for her own stamp. "Now I have to stamp the paper with my own mark," she explained, "and put the mark of this eagle in my own book."

Louise's rubber stamp was in the shape of a horseshoe. She pressed it against a little ink pad, then stamped the horseshoe mark to the paper. "There!" she said, blowing gently to dry the paper. "Now we can move on."

"Better put the box back carefully," Mandy said.

When the box was safely wedged back into the crevice, they began to retrace their steps, puzzling over the clue as they went. Abby, who had been distracted by the discovery of the first letterbox, now began to look around again, a nervous expression on her face.

"This is fun," Mandy said. "I'll bet we're going to find the second box in no time."

"I don't know about that," Louise said thoughtfully.

"It's a confusing sort of clue. How are we going to know when we've walked a mile?"

"When we see the post!" Mandy declared. She felt full of confidence now that they had found their first letter-box.

Louise didn't look convinced.

The journey back to Sittaford Tor passed quickly, and soon the massive stone-topped hill loomed over them. In spite of the low cloud and drizzle, the air was warm and muggy.

"I'm hot," said Abby.

"We can't give up," Louise chided. "Not after finding only one box!"

"No, let's keep going," Mandy said quickly.

"But we don't know where to begin!" Abby complained.

"Let's split up, then," suggested Lou. "We're not too far from home now, so we won't get lost. You go with Abby, Mandy, because she knows this area pretty well."

"Right," said Mandy. "Let's spread out, heading north. If we find a post, then we'll shout."

"Okay." Louise hurried ahead, and Mandy walked along with Abby, hoping the rain would hold off until they found their buried treasure.

They talked about what sort of post it could be — a

telegraph pole, or perhaps a wooden signpost. Watching carefully for a clue, neither of them noticed that a thick rolling fog had come swirling across the moor, smothering the moorland around them like a great gray blanket.

Mandy glanced up and let out a shout of dismay. "I didn't see it coming!"

"Neither did I," said Abby in a small voice. She linked arms with Mandy and they stopped.

"Which way?" Mandy prompted, looking at Abby.

Abby turned to the right, then to the left, then straight ahead again. Visibility was down to just a few yards. Everything seemed suddenly to have lost its recognizable shape, as though someone had taken an eraser to the landscape. Outlines of trees and bushes looked shifting and shadowy. It was horribly disorienting.

Abby clung a little tighter to Mandy's arm. "I don't know which way to go," she admitted. "I can't see."

"Oh, no," Mandy said, half to herself. Then, more brightly, she said, "Well, we'll shout for Lou. She can't be far away."

They began to call, each in turn, and then together. But there was no answering call.

"Louise knows this part of the moor better than I do," Abby confessed miserably.

"We've got two choices," said Mandy. "We can sit down and wait for the fog to lift, or we can walk in whichever direction you think is best."

Abby shivered. "It's creepy out here," she said. "Let's just keep moving. That way." She pointed to the path ahead, and they began to walk slowly forward, their arms linked. For a while, neither of them spoke. It was so completely silent that Mandy felt as if the two of them were the only people left in the world. She was about to suggest to Abby that they sing something to keep cheerful, when, drifting out of the gloom ahead, Curiosity appeared.

Ten

Abby froze. She stared at Mandy, her eyes wide. "It's Curiosity!" she whispered.

"It's okay, Abby," Mandy said. "We're not in danger." She paused, silently willing Curiosity to come closer. Even if Abby still didn't trust the foal, Mandy believed that she meant them no harm. She could hear a faint sucking sound as the small hooves came through the mud toward them.

They waited. The mud oozed around their shoes, and the fog reached out and touched their faces with damp fingers of mist. Mandy's excitement mounted as each second passed. Then the swirling mist parted, and Curiosity stood before them. Mandy could clearly make out just the shape of her fine, small head, her ears pricked forward, listening. Then she saw her eyes. Just as before, the foal looked directly at them, unblinking and unafraid. Mandy felt Abby tense.

"Oh, Curiosity!" she whispered.

"Hello, little friend," Mandy said softly. She was thrilled to see the foal again. She moved a step closer, then another, dragging Abby with her. With every step she could feel Abby's reluctance.

"Oh, please . . . let's go, let's just *go*!" she pleaded in a whisper.

"*Look*, Abby," Mandy said, her voice firm. "Look at the gentle expression in her eyes! You can't possibly think she wants to hurt us. Think about it, Abby. Curiosity loved you, didn't she? Don't you think she might have come back to see if you are all right?"

The foal tossed her mane and shook her head. Then she pawed delicately at the ground in front of her and deliberately turned away from them. With a swish of her tail, she began to trot lightly away. The curtain of fog opened, and she was gone.

"Oh, dear," Mandy muttered. "She's vanished again."

But Curiosity returned almost at once and stood looking pointedly at them. Then once again she pawed the ground, turned, and trotted away into the mist. She repeated the ritual a third time, and Mandy was mystified. What could it mean?

It was Abby who came up with an idea. "She wants us to follow her!" she gasped.

"You're right!" Mandy cried. "We must follow her, Abby. We *must*."

"Oh, no, Mandy," protested Abby. "We don't know where she might lead us!"

"Let's go with her," Mandy begged. "Then you'll see there's nothing to be afraid of."

Abby straightened and took a deep breath. "Okay," she agreed with a heavy sigh. "Okay, I'll do it. But I don't like it."

They set out after the foal, walking close together. Curiosity walked ahead, looking back from time to time as if to check that they were still behind her. She seemed impatient. There was a new urgency about her that puzzled Mandy. Mandy's heart thudded with expectation. She knew she was close to finding out what Curiosity wanted from them.

On they went across the moor. Neither of them had any idea where they were. Mandy was pretty certain that they were thoroughly lost, but somehow she trusted Curiosity not to lead them into danger. Once the foal stopped, and Mandy saw her dip her head and sniff the ground. Then, glancing behind at the girls, she skirted a piece of ground Mandy was sure was a carpet bog. The ground bubbled and heaved as the girls walked past it.

"See?" Mandy whispered to Abby. "Did you *see* that? That has to be proof that she's taking care of us. If she wanted to hurt us, she would have taken us straight through the middle of that bog!"

For the first time, Abby's frightened face relaxed. "Well, I guess you're right," she said. She looked down for a moment. "You're right, Mandy," she went on quietly. "Curiosity did love me as much as I loved her. If she really doesn't blame me for the accident, then maybe she *still* loves me."

Mandy reached over and squeezed Abby's hand. Then she looked around. "I wonder where we are," she said. "Do you have any idea?"

"None," Abby confessed, shaking her head. "My dad's going to be so angry if he finds out about us going off in the fog. We should have gone straight home, Mandy!"

"Well, we couldn't, could we? I mean, we were lost. Anyway, we'll be fine," Mandy said. "Curiosity will see to that."

When it seemed Mandy and Abby had slowed their pace, Curiosity waited, looking back over her shoulder, silently urging them on. There was such gentle encouragement in her eyes, Mandy's heart melted. "Look, Abby!" Mandy interrupted. "She's stopped."

Up ahead of them, the foal was standing stock-still, but this time she was not looking back at Mandy and Abby. She was gazing straight ahead, her delicate head held high and her nostrils flared.

"Come on, Abby," Mandy urged. "Let's see what she's looking at." She let go of Abby's arm and began to jog forward. Frowning into the fog, Mandy realized she had come right to the edge of a large area of mossy plants, bobbing on a stretch of dark, peaty water. Standing there, frozen to the spot, she heard a sound that sent a shiver of fear creeping along her spine.

She could hear something breathing! It was rasping, anguished breathing, reaching out to her from the brooding silence of this huge bog. Then there came the sound of a feeble splashing.

Mandy's insides churned, and her heart clenched tight in her chest. Something was in the bog! She looked around frantically for Curiosity, but she was nowhere to be seen. Mandy felt suddenly lost without her calm and reassuring presence. She turned. "Abby!" she shouted. "Quickly! Something needs our help."

"What is it?" asked Abby, arriving wide-eyed at Mandy's side. "Oh, it's a carpet bog! Don't take another step!" She clutched at Mandy, staring down at her feet.

"Listen!" Mandy hissed. They waited, hardly breathing. The splashing sound came again, followed by a pitiful neighing. The piercing whinny rang around them again and again, echoing through the fog. It was the same desperate cry Mandy had heard in Scorhill Stone Circle.

"Can you hear it?" Mandy asked urgently.

"Yes!" Abby looked alarmed. She stared out over the bog. "Is it Curiosity? Has she fallen into the bog?" Abby's face had turned chalk white.

"It can't be. . . ." Mandy felt helpless. What could they do? Out of nowhere a gusty little breeze started to blow. It tugged at the fog shrouding the surface of the bog and lifted it away.

Lying in the murky water was a tiny foal. Though it was submerged to the chest, Mandy could see that it was younger than Curiosity. Its head was propped against a large stone. One tiny hoof emerged from the bog and struck out at the dark water that held it prisoner.

"A *foal*!" she breathed. "It's trapped in the bog. We've got to do something!"

"But we can't!" Abby whispered. "It's too dangerous."

"We can," Mandy said firmly. "It's close to the edge of the bog. We can do it!"

"I think we should go for help," Abby said nervously.

"There's no time for that," Mandy reasoned. "Besides, we don't even know where we are."

"What are we going to do!" said Abby. "How are we going to get it out?"

Mandy looked around her. As the breeze chased away the fog, the sky had lightened. She was able to make out a few scrubby bushes and the slope of a hill some distance away. Where the boggy water pooled against stony ground, a log was lying. "Come on! We can use that log."

It took all of Mandy's strength to lift one end of it. Abby heaved at the other end. It was wider at her end, and just long enough to make a bridge out to where the foal lay.

Abby groaned. "This is really heavy."

They dragged the log across to the bog, then rolled it onto the spongy moss. Using the tip of her shoe, Mandy pushed the big piece of wood until it floated free of the ground at one end. Then it sank a little and came to rest on the muddy bottom, just as she had hoped. The bog water lapped around it, leaving a small island of log clear of the water.

"Let's hope it doesn't sink," Abby said. She hopped up onto the log, testing it for stability. It rolled slightly but sank no farther into the murky depths of the water. She stepped back onto the firm ground and nodded to

Mandy without speaking. Mandy gave a small smile and climbed onto the log. Abby followed her, her arms outstretched for balance.

The foal rolled its eyes as they stepped carefully along the log toward it. Mandy's heart was thumping so hard she was sure it would explode. She reached the end of the log and stretched down toward the terrified foal. It flailed at the water with one small leg, frantic to escape.

"We won't hurt you, little one," Mandy said soothingly. "Lie still. We're trying to help." Hoping she could keep her balance, she crouched down at the wider end of the log. Behind her, Abby did the same. They grasped the foal tightly and pulled. Mandy's arms were in the cold, peaty water up to her elbows, while Abby dug her hands into the foal's mane.

"Heave!" said Mandy, desperate to free the foal.

"I'm heaving," Abby puffed.

Again and again they tugged at the frightened animal, grabbing at any bit of its body they could find. The water was cold and slimy, and things Mandy couldn't identify plastered themselves against her skin. Once when she looked up, she felt strangely relieved to see Curiosity solemnly looking on. She stood on the dry slope on the far side of the bog, and Mandy sensed her encouragement. Curiosity was silently willing them to succeed in saving the life of the foal.

"We're going to save you," Mandy whispered to the foal in the bog. "I promise you we will." With renewed determination, she gave a tremendous pull. The foal's mud-encrusted body began to slide free.

"Oh!" gasped Abby. "Oh, Mandy! I think we've done it." Murky brown water splashed Abby's cheeks, mingling with the splattered slime and mud.

Now that he had been freed from the weeds and ooze

at the bottom of the bog, the foal seemed featherlight. It scrambled to its legs, took a few steps along the mossy green plants that grew above the water, and fell down.

Mandy and Abby began to shuffle backward down the log. The foal staggered about weakly until he reached firm ground. He was covered in muddy slime, but Mandy could just make out a dark blue-gray coat under all the dirt. The foal shook himself like a wet dog and stood shivering, blinking at Mandy and Abby.

"Oh, poor little thing," said Abby, who was still out of breath. "He's in a terrible state! We must get him home right away."

"Yes," said Mandy, her heart going out to the bedraggled foal. "He needs feeding and cleaning. Do you think he belongs to anybody?"

"I have no idea," Abby said. "But that doesn't matter right now. He needs help. Let's give him a minute to rest, then we'll see if we can get him to walk with us."

Mandy nodded. The foal was standing, though he was still a little unsteady on his hooves. His head hung low, and he showed no signs of wanting to bolt away across the moor.

Abby began inching toward him, speaking very gently as she did so. "It's all right now, little one, you're safe with us," she murmured. "We're going to take care of you." The foal lifted his head and looked at her, then stretched out his muzzle to sniff at her outstretched hand.

Mandy took a moment to look around for Curiosity. The skewbald foal was still watching them. She had moved along the bank of the bog and now began to paw purposefully at the ground. She swished her tail and turned her back.

"Look, Abby," Mandy said softly. She pointed to where Curiosity was standing. "That's our signal. She wants us to follow."

"She's going to lead us home," Abby said, sounding both surprised and relieved.

"Well," said Mandy, scrambling after Curiosity, "we'd better follow her. Come on!"

The foal walked slowly beside them. His breathing was wheezy, and he was lame in one back leg. But he plodded along determinedly, never leaving their side.

"He trusts us," Abby said happily. "He seems to know we're going to take care of him. Isn't he special?" Her eyes were shining.

"He is." Mandy smiled. "Really special." She was eager to get the foal back to the farm where he could be properly cared for.

"You were right to trust her," Abby said as they walked slowly along. "Curiosity, I mean." She put her hand lightly on the neck of the soggy little foal.

Mandy nodded, concentrating on the swish of Curiosity's tail up ahead. She was determined not to get lost again.

"I wish I could have understood her right from the start, like you," Abby went on.

"I just can't believe that any animal *means* to hurt someone," Mandy explained. "And Curiosity always seemed so gentle. You know, I think she knew about this foal all along."

A hazy sunshine was now pressing through the cloud. The moor had some definition to it. They followed Curiosity from the bog to where the landmarks on the moor started to look familiar to Abby.

"There's the road to the reservoir," she cried. "We were close to home after all."

At a fork in the road, Curiosity halted. She raised her head and looked directly at them, turning her dark, liquid eyes on each in turn. Mandy guessed that this would be the point at which she would leave them. Sadness welled up inside her at the thought of saying a final good-bye to the brave foal.

Abby stopped, then nudged Mandy in the ribs. "She's

going," she said softly, her eyes never leaving Curiosity's.

"I think so," Mandy agreed. A lump in her throat made it difficult to say anything else.

"Oh, Mandy, I'm going to miss her. It's still hard to say good-bye," Abby murmured.

"She'll rest more easily now," Mandy whispered. "She deserves that."

"Yes," Abby answered. "You're right. Good-bye, Curiosity. Good-bye, little friend."

The foal tossed her head and wheeled around. Then she broke into a spirited trot. Within seconds, Curiosity had vanished among the folds of the moor. Mandy knew it was the last they would see of her.

"Oh, my *goodness*!" exclaimed Mrs. Taylor as Abby described how she and Mandy had hauled the foal out of the bog. They were sitting in the kitchen at Sittaford Farm waiting for Louise and her parents and Mandy's to arrive.

"You were right not to try to walk into that water," Mr. Taylor said approvingly. "Good idea, using that log."

Mandy smiled at him. It had been a great relief seeing the foal settled into a bed of thick straw. They had washed off the worst of the mud and given him a bucketful of bran mash and molasses. When they had left the stall, the foal was dozing, his long legs tucked under him and his nose resting on the straw. He was beautiful, with a pearly dark-gray coat and a black mane and tail.

"Can I keep him, Dad?" Abby said now, her radiant face turned first to her father, then her mother. "Please?"

A wide grin spread over Mr. Taylor's face. "So you're ready to have a pony of your own again, Abby?"

"No question." The girl smiled.

"We'll ask around and find out whom he belongs to," said Mrs. Taylor. "Hopefully, he's for sale."

"Will-o'-the-wisp," said Abby, already certain the foal would be hers. "That's what I'll call him."

"That's really pretty," said Mandy. "What does it mean?"

"It's the blue flame we sometimes see on the peat marshes here. It's caused by gases that occur in the bogs."

"You could call him Willow, for short," Mandy suggested.

"That's pretty!" Abby grinned. She went over and gave Mandy a hug. "Thanks," she said.

"For what?" Mandy looked surprised.

"For sticking by me," Abby said simply. Neither of them had said a word about Curiosity's part in their adventure. They didn't need to. She was a wonderful secret, one they would keep forever.

That night while Louise was sleeping, Mandy crept to the open window and looked out to where a pale, round moon lit up the moor. The brooding silence made her shiver. And then she remembered the determined young foal who had come dancing toward her through the fog, driven by concern for her grief-stricken owner. Mandy remembered the foal's kind eyes and her wonderful courage — and wished her well with all her heart.

"Willow is safe now, Curiosity," she whispered. "Abby is going to take good care of him. You don't need to worry about him anymore."

TM

*Read more about Mandy's animal adventures
in the new Animal Ark™ book*

CATS AT THE CAMPGROUND

Mandy Hope gazed down at Dylan, the sick puppy who had been brought into Animal Ark the day before. "You're being such a brave boy," she said softly, stroking the puppy's head.

The young Bernese mountain dog, who was recovering from an operation on his spine, looked up at Mandy with soulful brown eyes. He was only four months old and still had his fluffy puppy coat. Mandy smoothed his silky black ears and lightly touched each of his sweet tan eyebrows.

Just then, the door opened. Dr. Emily Hope, Mandy's

mother, came in. "How is he?" she asked quietly. Her long red hair was tied back but, as usual, soft strands were escaping around her face.

"He's still not moving," Mandy replied, her blue eyes full of worry. "He *is* going to get better, isn't he, Mom?"

Dr. Emily leaned into Dylan's cage and gently examined the row of stitches that ran down the back of the pup's neck. "I hope so, love. I really do," she replied. "But it's going to be a few days before your dad and I know whether the operation has been a success."

"What would have happened if you hadn't operated?" Mandy asked, looking at the doleful puppy.

"His condition would have deteriorated quickly," her mom explained. "He had a cyst — a swelling — growing in his spine. It was stopping his muscles from getting the right messages from his brain. If we hadn't operated, then it would have gotten bigger, eventually paralyzing him." She stroked the puppy gently as she spoke. "It was a complicated operation, but if we hadn't done it, then Dylan would have had to be put to sleep. At least, this way, we've given him a chance."

Mandy nodded, feeling a little better.

"Let's leave him to rest, love," Dr. Emily said. "There's nothing more we can do now."

Giving Dylan a kiss on his head, Mandy shut the cage door. She followed her mom out of the residential unit where all the Animal Ark patients that were too ill to go home were kept. Animal Ark, an old stone cottage with a modern red-brick extension, was both Mandy's home and her parents' veterinary clinic.

"Now, didn't you say something about visiting Wilfred Bennett and Matty this morning?" Dr. Emily said as they went into the cozy, oak-beamed kitchen.

"Yes," said Mandy, taking off the white coat she always wore when she was helping with the patients. She cheered up slightly as she thought of her plans for the first day of spring break. "I'm meeting James at the Fox and Goose crossroads at ten o'clock, and then we're going on to Wilfred's house." Wilfred Bennett had once run the local riding school. A short while ago, his wife, Rose, had died and Wilfred had been forced to close the school. He had sold all of the horses, apart from Rose's gray mare, Matty, who was Mandy's favorite.

"Well, give Matty a hug from me," Dr. Emily said.

"And an apple?" said Mandy, looking hopefully at the large fruit bowl on the kitchen table.

Her mom smiled. "And an apple," she said.

"Thanks, Mom," Mandy said, pulling on a jacket and stuffing the biggest apple into her pocket.

Dr. Emily glanced at her watch. "Did you just say you were meeting James at ten?"

Mandy nodded.

Her mother raised her eyebrows. "Well, you'd better get a move on. It's five minutes past already."

"Oh, no!" Mandy gasped. She had been so busy with Dylan that she had completely lost track of time. "James'll be mad!"

"Bye!" Dr. Emily laughed, as Mandy grabbed her scarf and ran out of the door.

It only took Mandy a few seconds to jump onto her bike. She pedaled furiously past the wooden sign that read ANIMAL ARK VETERINARY CLINIC and down the lane that led to the main road. A biting February wind blew Mandy's short, dark-blond hair back from her face, but she was cycling so hard that she hardly felt the cold.

As she got near the crossroads, she saw James Hunter, her best friend, and Blackie, his Labrador, waiting by the signpost. James was standing by his bike, his glasses halfway down his nose as usual.

"What time do you call this?" he said, pretending to be indignant, as Mandy braked beside him.

"Sorry," she panted, her cheeks flushed from the wind and exercise. She patted Blackie, who was leaping around her ecstatically. "I was with Dylan."

"Oh, how is he?" James asked quickly. Mandy had called him up the night before to tell him all about the puppy's operation.

"Still not moving," Mandy replied. Blackie jumped up

at her, almost sending her and her bike flying. "Blackie!" she said sternly. "Down!"

Blackie backed off. Mandy quickly stroked him to show that she didn't mean to be cross with him. She had known Blackie ever since he had been a tiny puppy and she adored him. As she scratched his ears, he thumped his tail against the ground. "He's frisky today," she said to James.

"He hasn't been for a walk yet," James said. He looked rather sheepish. "Actually, I overslept — I only got here about a minute ago."

"And you let *me* feel guilty!" Mandy exclaimed, reaching out to punch his arm.

James dodged and grinned. "I couldn't resist it! Come on, let's go. If we cycle fast, it might tire Blackie out."

They biked along the hilly road that led out of Welford village, with Blackie bounding happily beside them. The tree branches were still bare but along the roadside there were clumps of nodding white snowdrops and the first early daffodils could just be seen pushing their green tips out of the ground.

Wilfred Bennett's small stone cottage stood by the roadside just outside the village. The rolling land behind it, which had once been Wilfred's riding school, was now fenced off and a sign by the entrance leading into it read ROSE OF YORKSHIRE CAMPSITE.

"I wonder when the campsite will be opening again

for the summer," Mandy said to James as they leaned their bikes against the fence.

"Maybe Wilfred will know," James said. He called Blackie, who was sniffing in some long grass. Blackie trotted over and sat obediently to have his leash clipped onto his collar. "There, you're not naughty all the time, are you?" James said, glancing at Mandy.

She grinned. "Just most of it!"

They went to Wildred's front door and banged the horse-shaped brass knocker. A few moments later, the door opened and Wilfred Bennett's kind old face peered out.

"Hi, Wilfred," Mandy said. "We've come to visit."

Wilfred's weather-beaten cheeks creased even more as he smiled broadly. "Well, that's what I call a coincidence," he said in his deep Yorkshire accent. "I was going to give you two a call this morning. I've got a little problem and I thought you might be able to help."

"What is it?" James asked curiously.

But before Wilfred could reply, a thin gray cat came trotting around the corner of the cottage. Mandy looked at it in surprise. Wilfred didn't have a cat.

Suddenly, Blackie spotted the cat, too. With an excited bark, he lunged forward, almost pulling James off his feet.

The cat froze for half a second and then, like lightning, it streaked across the road and vanished under the far hedge in a blur of dark gray fur.

"Blackie!" James cried. "How many times have I told you not to do that?"

Blackie sat down again, looking contrite. But Mandy grinned as she noticed a slight wag in the Labrador's tail. She turned to Wilfred. "Whose cat is that?" she asked. "I haven't seen it before."

"I don't rightly know," Wilfred replied. "But it's my guess she was one of Arthur Oldfield's cats."

"Oh! Poor thing!" Mandy gasped. She had heard her parents talking about Arthur Oldfield a while ago. He had been a bit of a recluse, his only company being the handful of pedigree British Blue cats he kept. But last summer he died, and his distraught pets had run off and begun to live wild.

Wilfred nodded gravely. "I've seen several gray cats like his around here," he added. "That one turned up yesterday and made a home in my backyard." He rubbed his chin. "I put a little food out for her," he said. "But the problem is, I'm allergic to cats, so I'd like it if she found another home. That's why I was going to call you. I thought you might be able to help," he explained.

"Of course we will," Mandy said immediately. She and James had often rescued stray animals before — dogs, cats, and all sorts of wildlife. But her parents had a strict rule about taking in stray animals at Animal Ark. "We have enough animal responsibilities as it is," her mom always said. However, Mandy was sure that kind-hearted Betty Hilder, who ran the nearby animal sanctuary, would be happy to take the cat.

Already Mandy's mind was whirling, but before she could say anything else, Wilfred spoke again. "Before you do anything, I think there's something else you should see . . ." he said.

Exchanging surprised glances, Mandy and James followed Wilfred into his backyard. What was he going to show them?

Wilfred's backyard was tiny, only little more than a square of concrete containing a trash can and a coal bin. He led them across the yard to where a narrow passageway ran between the cottage and the campsite fence. He nodded at the passageway. "There," he said.

Mandy stepped forward. The passageway was half covered by the overhanging roof of the cottage and at the far end it was shadowy and dimly lit. She could just make out a pile of old newspapers and there in the newspapers were . . .

"Kittens!" she gasped.

Huddled together in a makeshift newspaper nest were three small kittens. Two were gray and white and one was black with a white triangle on its chest. They crouched together, their eyes blinking. From the size of them, Mandy guessed they must be three to four weeks old. She swung around. "Are they the gray cat's?"

"Yes," Wilfred said, nodding. "She brought them here yesterday. It's my guess she was looking for somewhere safe for them, but they can't stay here — it's too cold. They need to be inside."

Blackie pulled on his leash, whining in his eagerness to go and investigate the kittens. They shrank back nervously against the paper, making tiny meowing sounds.

"I'd better keep Blackie away from them," James said quickly. "He might scare them."

Mandy nodded. "I'll see how friendly they are," she said. She edged cautiously into the narrow passageway. The kittens drew back a little. Careful not to alarm them, Mandy crouched down and crawled slowly on her knees toward them. The ground was damp but Mandy didn't care. Her eyes were fixed on the three kittens.

As she drew closer, she could see their markings more clearly. Both gray-and-white kittens had gray heads and white chests, but one was smaller than the other and had a white smudge on its muzzle and white front legs. The third kitten was jet-black apart from the white triangle on its chest and four white paws. They stared at her, their eyes huge in their skinny faces, their pointed ears standing upright.

"Here, little ones," Mandy murmured, stopping and holding out her hand. "I'm not going to hurt you."

The black kitten ventured forward a few steps; he was still so young that his movements were uncoordinated and his legs unsteady.

Mandy stayed still and waited. "Come on," she coaxed softly. "It's OK."

The black kitten wobbled closer. Very slowly, Mandy reached out and tickled him under his chin. He opened his mouth and meowed loudly.

Mandy smiled. He was absolutely adorable. Hearing his meow, the other two kittens began to come toward her. They were too young to have any real fear of humans and soon they were crowding around her as she stroked and tickled them. The little female was shivering slightly and all three of them felt cold.

"They seem very friendly," James said from the entrance to the passageway.

Mandy looked around. "They are." Reluctantly, she placed them back in their nest and backed out. "But we've got to get them somewhere warm and dry." She stroked Blackie, who was sniffing eagerly at the kitten smell on her jeans.

"Here's the mother," Wilfred said softly, nodding at the yard entrance.

James immediately tightened his hold on Blackie's

leash. Seeing them, the mother cat stopped in her tracks.

"It's all right," Mandy said, crouching down. "We won't hurt you."

But the cat didn't seem to believe her. Turning on the spot, she fled back through the gate.